The Secret of the Island

The Secret of the Island

Jules Verne
(translation from
W.H.G. Kingston)

MINT EDITIONS

The Secret of the Island was first published in 1875.

This edition published by Mint Editions 2021.

ISBN 9781513271286 | E-ISBN 9781513276281

Published by Mint Editions®

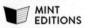 MINT
EDITIONS

minteditionbooks.com

Publishing Director: Jennifer Newens
Design & Production: Rachel Lopez Metzger
Project Manager: Micaela Clark
This book is a translation from the French original by Jules Verne.
Typesetting: Westchester Publishing Services

Contents

I

Lost or saved—Ayrton summoned—Important Discussion—
It is not the Duncan—Suspicious Vessel—Precautions to
be taken—The Ship approaches—A Cannon-Shot—The Brig
anchors in Sight of the Island—Night comes on.

It was now two years and a half since the castaways from the balloon had been thrown on Lincoln Island, and during that period there had been no communication between them and their fellow-creatures. Once the reporter had attempted to communicate with the inhabited world by confiding to a bird a letter which contained the secret of their situation, but that was a chance on which it was impossible to reckon seriously. Ayrton, alone, under the circumstances which have been related, had come to join the little colony. Now, suddenly, on this day, the 17th of October, other men had unexpectedly appeared in sight of the island, on that deserted sea!

There could be no doubt about it! A vessel was there! But would she pass on, or would she put into port? In a few hours the colonists would definitely know what to expect.

Cyrus Harding and Herbert having immediately called Gideon Spilett, Pencroft, and Neb into the dining-room of Granite House, told them what had happened. Pencroft, seizing the telescope, rapidly swept the horizon, and stopping on the indicated point, that is to say, on that which had made the almost imperceptible spot on the photographic negative—

"I'm blessed but it is really a vessel!" he exclaimed, in a voice which did not express any great amount of satisfaction.

"Is she coming here?" asked Gideon Spilett.

"Impossible to say anything yet," answered Pencroft, "for her rigging alone is above the horizon, and not a bit of her hull can be seen."

"What is to be done?" asked the lad.

"Wait," replied Harding.

And for a considerable time the settlers remained silent, given up to all the thoughts, all the emotions, all the fears, all the hopes, which were aroused by this incident—the most important which had occurred since their arrival in Lincoln Island. Certainly, the colonists were not in the situation of castaways abandoned on a sterile islet, constantly contending against a cruel nature for their miserable existence, and incessantly tormented by the longing to return to inhabited countries. Pencroft and Neb, especially, who felt themselves at once so happy and so rich, would not have left their island without regret. They were accustomed, besides, to this new life in the midst of the domain which their intelligence had as it were civilised. But at any rate this ship brought news from the world, perhaps even from their native land. It was bringing fellow-creatures to them, and it may be conceived how deeply their hearts were moved at the sight!

From time to time Pencroft took the glass and rested himself at the window. From thence he very attentively examined the vessel, which was at a distance of twenty miles to the east. The colonists had as yet, therefore, no means of signalising their presence. A flag would not have been perceived; a gun would not have been heard; a fire would not have been visible. However, it was certain that the island, overtopped by Mount Franklin, could not have escaped the notice of the vessel's look-out. But why was this ship coming there? Was it simple chance which brought it to that part of the Pacific, where the maps mentioned no land except Tabor Islet, which itself was out of the route usually followed by vessels from the Polynesian Archipelagos, from New Zealand, and from the American coast? To this question, which each one asked himself, a reply was suddenly made by Herbert.

"Can it be the *Duncan*?" he cried.

The *Duncan*, as has been said, was Lord Glenarvan's yacht, which had left Ayrton on the islet, and which was to return there some day to fetch him. Now, the islet was not so far-distant from Lincoln Island, but that a vessel, standing for the one, could pass in sight of the other. A hundred and fifty miles only separated them in longitude, and seventy in latitude.

"We must tell Ayrton," said Gideon Spilett, "and send for him immediately. He alone can say if it is the *Duncan*."

This was the opinion of all, and the reporter, going to the telegraphic apparatus which placed the corral in communication with Granite House, sent this telegram:—"Come with all possible speed."

In a few minutes the bell sounded.

"I am coming," replied Ayrton.

Then the settlers continued to watch the vessel.

"If it is the *Duncan*," said Herbert, "Ayrton will recognise her without difficulty, since he sailed on board her for some time."

JULES VERNE (TRANSLATION FROM W.H.G. KINGSTON)

"And if he recognises her," added Pencroft, "it will agitate him exceedingly!"

"Yes," answered Cyrus Harding; "but now Ayrton is worthy to return on board the *Duncan*, and pray Heaven that it is indeed Lord Glenarvan's yacht, for I should be suspicious of any other vessel. These are ill-famed seas, and I have always feared a visit from Malay pirates to our island."

"We could defend it," cried Herbert.

"No doubt, my boy," answered the engineer smiling, "but it would be better not to have to defend it."

"A useless observation," said Spilett. "Lincoln Island is unknown to navigators, since it is not marked even on the most recent maps. Do you not think, Cyrus, that that is a sufficient motive for a ship, finding herself unexpectedly in sight of new land, to try and visit rather than avoid it?"

"Certainly," replied Pencroft.

"I think so too," added the engineer. "It may even be said that it is the duty of a captain to come and survey any land or island not yet known, and Lincoln Island is in this position."

"Well," said Pencroft, "suppose this vessel comes and anchors there a few cables-lengths from our island, what shall we do?" This sudden question remained at first without any reply. But Cyrus Harding, after some moments' thought, replied in the calm tone which was usual to him—

"What we shall do, my friends? What we ought to do is this:—we will communicate with the ship, we will take our passage on board her, and we will leave our island, after having taken possession of it in the name of the United States. Then we will return with any who may wish to follow us to colonise it definitely, and endow the American Republic with a useful station in this part of the Pacific Ocean!"

"Hurrah!" exclaimed Pencroft, "and that will be no small present which we shall make to our country! The colonisation is already almost finished; names are given to every part of the island; there is a natural port, fresh water, roads, a telegraph, a dockyard, and manufactories; and there will be nothing to be done but to inscribe Lincoln Island on the maps!"

"But if any one seizes it in our absence?" observed Gideon Spilett.

"Hang it!" cried the sailor. "I would rather remain all alone to guard it: and trust to Pencroft, they shouldn't steal it from him, like a watch from the pocket of a swell!"

For an hour it was impossible to say with any certainty whether the vessel was or was not standing towards Lincoln Island. She was nearer, but in what direction was she sailing? This Pencroft could not determine. However, as the wind was blowing from the north-east, in all probability the vessel was sailing on the starboard tack. Besides, the wind was favourable for bringing her towards the island, and, the sea being calm, she would not be afraid to approach although the shallows were not marked on the chart.

Towards four o'clock—an hour after he had been sent for—Ayrton arrived at Granite House. He entered the dining-room, saying—

"At your service, gentlemen."

Cyrus Harding gave him his hand, as was his custom to do, and, leading him to the window—

"Ayrton," said he, "we have begged you to come here for an important reason. A ship is in sight of the island."

Ayrton at first paled slightly, and for a moment his eyes became dim; then, leaning out of the window, he surveyed the horizon, but could see nothing.

"Take this telescope," said Spilett, "and look carefully, Ayrton, for it is possible that this ship may be the *Duncan* come to these seas for the purpose of taking you home again."

"The *Duncan*!" murmured Ayrton. "Already?" This last word escaped Ayrton's lips as if involuntarily, and his head drooped upon his hands.

Did not twelve years' solitude on a desert island appear to him a sufficient expiation? Did not the penitent yet feel himself pardoned, either in his own eyes or in the eyes of others?

"No," said he, "no! it cannot be the *Duncan*!"

"Look, Ayrton," then said the engineer, "for it is necessary that we should know beforehand what to expect."

Ayrton took the glass and pointed it in the direction indicated. During some minutes he examined the horizon without moving, without uttering a word. Then—

"It is indeed a vessel," said he, "but I do not think she is the *Duncan*."

"Why do you not think so?" asked Gideon Spilett. "Because the *Duncan* is a steam-yacht, and I cannot perceive any trace of smoke either above or near that vessel."

"Perhaps she is simply sailing," observed Pencroft. "The wind is favourable for the direction which she appears to be taking, and she may be anxious to economise her coal, being so far from land."

"It is possible that you may be right, Mr. Pencroft," answered Ayrton, "and that the vessel has extinguished her fires. We must wait until she is nearer, and then we shall soon know what to expect."

So saying, Ayrton sat down in a corner of the room and remained silent. The colonists again discussed the strange ship, but Ayrton took no part in the conversation. All were in such a mood that they found it impossible to continue their work. Gideon Spilett and Pencroft were particularly nervous, going, coming, not able to remain still in one place. Herbert felt more curiosity. Neb alone maintained his usual calm manner. Was not his country that where his master was? As to the engineer, he remained plunged in deep thought, and in his heart feared rather than desired the arrival of the ship. In the meanwhile, the vessel was a little nearer the island. With the aid of the glass, it was ascertained that she was a brig, and not one of those Malay proas, which are generally used by the pirates of the Pacific. It was, therefore, reasonable to believe that the engineer's apprehensions would not be justified, and that the presence of this vessel in the vicinity of the island was fraught with no danger. Pencroft, after a minute examination, was able positively to affirm that the vessel was rigged as a brig, and that she was standing obliquely towards the coast, on the starboard tack, under her topsails and topgallant-sails. This was confirmed by Ayrton. But by continuing in this direction she must soon disappear behind Claw Cape, as the wind was from the south-west, and to watch her it would be then necessary to ascend the heights of Washington Bay, near Port Balloon—a provoking circumstance, for it was already five o'clock in the evening, and the twilight would soon make any observation extremely difficult.

"What shall we do when night comes on?" asked Gideon Spilett. "Shall we light a fire, so as to signal our presence, on the coast?"

This was a serious question, and yet, although the engineer still retained some of his presentiments, it was answered in the affirmative. During the night the ship might disappear and leave for ever, and, this ship gone, would another ever return to the waters of Lincoln Island? Who could foresee what the future would then have in store for the colonists?

"Yes," said the reporter, "we ought to make known to that vessel, whoever she may be, that the island is inhabited. To neglect the opportunity which is offered to us might be to create everlasting regrets."

It was, therefore, decided that Neb and Pencroft should go to Port Balloon, and that there, at nightfall, they should light an immense fire, the blaze of which would necessarily attract the attention of the brig.

But at the moment when Neb and the sailor were preparing to leave Granite House, the vessel suddenly altered her course, and stood directly for Union Bay. The brig was a good sailer, for she approached rapidly. Neb and Pencroft put off their departure, therefore, and the glass was put into Ayrton's hands, that he might ascertain for certain whether the ship was or was not the *Duncan*. The Scotch yacht was also rigged as a brig. The question was, whether a chimney could be discerned between the two masts of the vessel, which was now at a distance of only five miles.

The horizon was still very clear. The examination was easy, and Ayrton soon let the glass fall again, saying—

"It is not the *Duncan*! It could not be her!"

Pencroft again brought the brig within the range of the telescope, and could see that she was of between three and four hundred tons burden, wonderfully narrow, well-masted, admirably built, and must be a very rapid sailer. But to what nation did she belong? That was difficult to say.

"And yet," added the sailor, "a flag is floating from her peak, but I cannot distinguish the colours of it."

"In half an hour we shall be certain about that," answered the reporter. "Besides, it is very evident that the intention of the captain of this ship is to land, and, consequently, if not to-day, to-morrow at the latest, we shall make his acquaintance."

"Never mind!" said Pencroft. "It is best to know whom we have to deal with, and I shall not be sorry to recognise that fellow's colours!"

And, while thus speaking, the sailor never left the glass. The day began to fade, and with the day the breeze fell also. The brig's ensign hung in folds, and it became more and more difficult to observe it.

"It is not the American flag," said Pencroft from time to time, "nor the English, the red of which could be easily seen, nor the French or German colours, nor the white flag of Russia, nor the yellow of Spain. One would say it was all one colour. Let's see: in these seas, what do we generally meet with? The Chilian flag?—but that is tri-colour. Brazilian?—it is green. Japanese?—it is yellow and black, whilst this—"

At that moment the breeze blew out the unknown flag. Ayrton, seizing the telescope which the sailor had put down, put it to his eye, and in a hoarse voice—

"The black flag!" he exclaimed.

And indeed the sombre bunting was floating from the mast of the brig, and they had now good reason for considering her to be a suspicious vessel!

Had the engineer, then, been right in his presentiments? Was this a pirate vessel? Did she scour the Pacific, competing with the Malay proas which still infest it? For what had she come to look at the shores of Lincoln Island? Was it to them an unknown island, ready to become a magazine for stolen cargoes? Had she come to find on the coast a sheltered port for the winter months? Was the settler's honest domain destined to be transformed into an infamous refuge—the headquarters of the piracy of the Pacific?

All these ideas instinctively presented themselves to the colonists' imaginations. There was no doubt, besides, of the signification which must be attached to the colour of the hoisted flag. It was that of pirates! It was that which the *Duncan* would have carried, had the convicts succeeded in their criminal design! No time was lost before discussing it.

"My friends," said Cyrus Harding, "perhaps this vessel only wishes to survey the coast of the island. Perhaps her crew will not land. There is a chance of it. However that may be, we ought to do everything we can to hide our presence here. The windmill on Prospect Heights is too easily seen. Let Ayrton and Neb go and take down the sails. We must also conceal the windows of Granite House with thick branches. All the fires must be extinguished, so that nothing may betray the presence of men on the island."

"And our vessel?" said Herbert.

"Oh," answered Pencroft, "she is sheltered in Port Balloon, and I defy any of those rascals there to find her!"

The engineer's orders were immediately executed. Neb and Ayrton ascended the plateau, and took the necessary precautions to conceal any indication of a settlement. Whilst they were thus occupied, their companions went to the border of Jacamar Wood, and brought back a large quantity of branches and creepers, which would at some distance appear as natural foliage, and thus disguise the windows in the granite cliff. At the same time, the ammunition and guns were placed ready so as to be at hand in case of an unexpected attack.

When all these precautions had been taken—

"My friends," said Harding, and his voice betrayed some emotion, "if these wretches endeavour to seize Lincoln Island, we shall defend it—shall we not?"

"Yes, Cyrus," replied the reporter, "and if necessary we will die to defend it!"

The engineer extended his hand to his companions, who pressed it warmly.

Ayrton alone remained in his corner, not joining the colonists. Perhaps he, the former convict, still felt himself unworthy to do so!

Cyrus Harding understood what was passing in Ayrton's mind, and going to him—

"And you, Ayrton," he asked, "what will you do?"

"My duty," answered Ayrton.

He then took up his station near the window and gazed through the foliage.

It was now half-past seven. The sun had disappeared twenty minutes ago behind Granite House. Consequently the eastern horizon was becoming gradually obscured. In the meanwhile the brig continued to advance towards Union Bay. She was now not more than two miles off, and exactly opposite the plateau of Prospect Heights, for after having tacked off Claw Cape, she had drifted towards the north in the current of the rising tide. One might have said that at this distance she had already entered the vast bay, for a straight line drawn from Claw Cape to Cape Mandible would have rested on her starboard quarter.

Was the brig about to penetrate far into the bay? That was the first question. When once in the bay, would she anchor there? That was the second. Would she not content herself with only surveying the coast, and stand out to sea again without landing her crew? They would know this in an hour. The colonists could do nothing but wait.

Cyrus Harding had not seen the suspected vessel hoist the black flag without deep anxiety. Was it not a direct menace against the work which he and his companions had till now conducted so successfully? Had these pirates—for the sailors of the brig could be nothing else— already visited the island, since on approaching it they had hoisted their colours. Had they formerly invaded it, so that certain unaccountable peculiarities might be explained in this way? Did there exist in the as yet unexplored parts some accomplice ready to enter into communication with them?

To all these questions which he mentally asked himself, Harding knew not what to reply; but he felt that the safety of the colony could not but be seriously threatened by the arrival of the brig.

However, he and his companions were determined to fight to the last gasp. It would have been very important to know if the pirates were numerous and better armed than the colonists. But how was this information to be obtained?

Night fell. The new moon had disappeared. Profound darkness enveloped the island and the sea. No light could pierce through the heavy piles of clouds on the horizon. The wind had died away completely with the twilight. Not a leaf rustled on the trees, not a ripple murmured on the shore. Nothing could be seen of the ship, all her lights being extinguished, and if she was still in sight of the island, her whereabouts could not be discovered.

"Well! who knows?" said Pencroft. "Perhaps that cursed craft will stand off during the night, and we shall see nothing of her at daybreak."

As if in reply to the sailor's observation, a bright light flashed in the darkness, and a cannon-shot was heard.

The vessel was still there and had guns on board.

Six seconds elapsed between the flash and the report.

Therefore the brig was about a mile and a quarter from the coast.

At the same time, the chains were heard rattling through the hawse-holes.

The vessel had just anchored in sight of Granite House!

II

There was no longer any doubt as to the pirates' intentions. They had dropped anchor at a short distance from the island, and it was evident that the next day by means of their boats they purposed to land on the beach!

Cyrus Harding and his companions were ready to act, but, determined though they were, they must not forget to be prudent. Perhaps their presence might still be concealed in the event of the pirates contenting themselves with landing on the shore without examining the interior of the island. It might be, indeed, that their only intention was to obtain fresh water from the Mercy, and it was not impossible that the bridge, thrown across a mile and a half from the mouth, and the manufactory at the Chimneys might escape their notice.

But why was that flag hoisted at the brig's peak? What was that shot fired for? Pure bravado doubtless, unless it was a sign of the act of taking possession. Harding knew now that the vessel was well-armed. And what had the colonists of Lincoln Island to reply to the pirates' guns? A few muskets only.

"However," observed Cyrus Harding, "here we are in an impregnable position. The enemy cannot discover the mouth of the outlet, now that it is hidden under reeds and grass, and consequently it would be impossible for them to penetrate into Granite House."

"But our plantations, our poultry-yard, our corral, all, everything!" exclaimed Pencroft, stamping his foot. "They may spoil everything, destroy everything in a few hours!"

"Everything, Pencroft," answered Harding, "and we have no means of preventing them."

"Are they numerous? that is the question," said the reporter. "If they are not more than a dozen, we shall be able to stop them, but forty, fifty, more perhaps!"

"Captain Harding," then said Ayrton, advancing towards the engineer, "will you give me leave."

"For what, my friend?"

"To go to that vessel to find out the strength of her crew."

"But Ayrton—" answered the engineer, hesitating, "you will risk your life—"

"Why not, sir?"

"That is more than your duty."

"I have more than my duty to do," replied Ayrton.

"Will you go to the ship in the boat?" asked Gideon Spilett.

"No, sir, but I will swim. A boat would be seen where a man may glide between wind and water."

"Do you know that the brig is a mile and a quarter from the shore?" said Herbert.

"I am a good swimmer, Mr. Herbert."

"I tell you it is risking your life," said the engineer.

"That is no matter," answered Ayrton. "Captain Harding, I ask this as a favour. Perhaps it will be a means of raising me in my own eyes!"

"Go, Ayrton," replied the engineer, who felt sure that a refusal would have deeply wounded the former convict, now become an honest man.

"I will accompany you," said Pencroft.

"You mistrust me!" said Ayrton quickly.

Then more humbly,—

"Alas!"

"No! no!" exclaimed Harding with animation, "no, Ayrton, Pencroft does not mistrust you. You interpret his words wrongly."

"Indeed," returned the sailor, "I only propose to accompany Ayrton as far as the islet. It may be, although it is scarcely possible, that one of these villains has landed, and in that case two men will not be too many to hinder him from giving the alarm. I will wait for Ayrton on the islet, and he shall go alone to the vessel, since he has proposed to do so." These things agreed to, Ayrton made preparations for his departure. His plan was bold, but it might succeed, thanks to the darkness of the night. Once arrived at the vessel's side, Ayrton, holding onto the main-chains, might reconnoitre the number and perhaps overhear the intentions of the pirates.

Ayrton and Pencroft, followed by their companions, descended to the beach. Ayrton undressed and rubbed himself with grease, so as to suffer less from the temperature of the water, which was still cold. He might, indeed, be obliged to remain in it for several hours.

Pencroft and Neb, during this time, had gone to fetch the boat, moored a few hundred feet higher up, on the bank of the Mercy, and by the time they returned, Ayrton was ready to start. A coat was thrown over his shoulders, and the settlers all came round him to press his hand.

Ayrton then shoved off with Pencroft in the boat.

It was half-past ten in the evening when the two adventurers disappeared in the darkness. Their companions returned to wait at the Chimneys.

The channel was easily traversed, and the boat touched the opposite shore of the islet. This was not done without precaution, for fear lest the pirates might be roaming about there. But after a careful survey, it was evident that the islet was deserted. Ayrton then, followed by Pencroft, crossed it with a rapid step, scaring the birds nestled in the holes of the rocks; then, without hesitating, he plunged into the sea, and swam noiselessly in the direction of the ship, in which a few lights had recently appeared, showing her exact situation. As to Pencroft, he crouched down in a cleft of the rock, and awaited the return of his companion.

In the meanwhile, Ayrton, swimming with a vigorous stroke, glided through the sheet of water without producing the slightest ripple. His head just emerged above it and his eyes were fixed on the dark hull of the brig, from which the lights were reflected in the water. He thought only of the duty which he had promised to accomplish, and nothing of the danger which he ran, not only on board the ship, but in the sea, often frequented by sharks. The current bore him along and he rapidly receded from the shore.

Half an hour afterwards, Ayrton, without having been either seen or heard, arrived at the ship and caught hold of the main-chains. He took breath, then, hoisting himself up, he managed to reach the extremity of the cutwater. There were drying several pairs of sailors' trousers. He put on a pair. Then settling himself firmly, he listened. They were not sleeping on board the brig. On the contrary, they were talking, singing, laughing. And these were the sentences, accompanied with oaths, which principally struck Ayrton:—

"Our brig is a famous acquisition."

"She sails well, and merits her name of the *Speedy*."

"She would show all the navy of Norfolk a clean pair of heels."

"Hurrah for her captain!"

"Hurrah for Bob Harvey!"

What Ayrton felt when he overheard this fragment of conversation may be understood when it is known that in this Bob Harvey he recognised one of his old Australian companions, a daring sailor, who had continued his criminal career. Bob Harvey had seized, on the shores of Norfolk Island, this brig, which was loaded with arms, ammunition, utensils, and tools of all sorts, destined for one of the Sandwich Islands. All his gang had gone on board, and pirates after having been convicts, these wretches, more ferocious than the Malays themselves, scoured the Pacific, destroying vessels, and massacring their crews.

The convicts spoke loudly, they recounted their deeds, drinking deeply at the same time, and this is what Ayrton gathered. The actual crew of the *Speedy* was composed solely of English prisoners, escaped from Norfolk Island.

Here it may be well to explain what this island was. In 29 degrees 2 minutes south latitude, and 165 degrees 42 minutes east longitude, to the east of Australia, is found a little island, six miles in circumference, overlooked by Mount Pitt, which rises to a height of 1100 feet above the level of the sea. This is Norfolk Island, once the seat of an establishment in which were lodged the most intractable convicts from the English penitentiaries. They numbered 500, under an iron discipline, threatened with terrible punishments, and were guarded by 150 soldiers, and 150 employed under the orders of the governor. It would be difficult to imagine a collection of greater ruffians. Sometimes,—although very rarely,—notwithstanding the extreme surveillance of which they were the object, many managed to escape, and seizing vessels which they surprised, they infested the Polynesian Archipelagos.

Thus had Bob Harvey and his companions done. Thus had Ayrton formerly wished to do. Bob Harvey had seized the brig *Speedy*, anchored in sight of Norfolk Island; the crew had been massacred; and for a year this ship had scoured the Pacific, under the command of Harvey, now a pirate, and well-known to Ayrton!

The convicts were, for the most part, assembled under the poop; but a few, stretched on the deck, were talking loudly.

The conversation still continued amidst shouts and libations. Ayrton learned that chance alone had brought the *Speedy* in sight of Lincoln Island: Bob Harvey had never yet set foot on it; but, as Cyrus Harding had conjectured, finding this unknown land in his course, its position being marked on no chart, he had formed the project of visiting it, and, if he found it suitable, of making it the brig's headquarters.

As to the black flag hoisted at the *Speedy's* peak, and the gun which had been fired, in imitation of men-of-war when they lower their colours, it was pure piratical bravado. It was in no way a signal, and no communication yet existed between the convicts and Lincoln Island.

The settlers' domain was now menaced with terrible danger. Evidently the island, with its water, its harbour, its resources of all kinds so increased in value by the colonists, and the concealment afforded by Granite House, could not but be convenient for the convicts; in their hands it would become an excellent place of refuge, and, being unknown, it would assure them, for a long time perhaps, impunity and security. Evidently, also, the lives of the settlers would not be respected, and Bob Harvey and his accomplices' first care would be to massacre them without mercy. Harding and his companions had, therefore, not even the choice of flying and hiding themselves in the island, since the convicts intended to reside there, and since, in the event of the *Speedy* departing on an expedition, it was probable that some of the crew would remain on shore, so as to settle themselves there. Therefore, it would be necessary to fight, to destroy every one of these scoundrels, unworthy of pity, and against whom any means would be right. So thought Ayrton, and he well knew that Cyrus Harding would be of his way of thinking.

But was resistance and, in the last place, victory possible? That would depend on the equipment of the brig, and the number of men which she carried.

This Ayrton resolved to learn at any cost, and as an hour after his arrival the vociferations had begun to die away, and as a large number of the convicts were already buried in a drunken sleep, Ayrton did not hesitate to venture onto the *Speedy's* deck, which the extinguished lanterns now left in total darkness. He hoisted himself onto the cutwater, and by the bowsprit arrived at the forecastle. Then, gliding among the convicts stretched here and there, he made the round of the ship, and found that the *Speedy* carried four guns, which would throw shot of from eight to ten pounds in weight. He found also, on touching them, that these guns were breech-loaders. They were, therefore, of modern make, easily used, and of terrible effect.

As to the men lying on the deck, they were about ten in number, but it was to be supposed that more were sleeping down below. Besides, by listening to them, Ayrton had understood that there were fifty on board. That was a large number for the six settlers of Lincoln Island to contend with! But now, thanks to Ayrton's devotion, Cyrus Harding would not be surprised, he would know the strength of his adversaries, and would make his arrangements accordingly.

There was nothing more for Ayrton to do but to return, and render to his companions an account of the mission with which he had charged himself, and he prepared to regain the bows of the brig, so that he might let himself down into the water.

But to this man, whose wish was, as he had said, to do more than his duty, there came an heroic thought. This was to sacrifice his own life, but save the island and the colonists. Cyrus Harding evidently could not resist fifty ruffians, all well-armed, who, either by penetrating by main force into Granite House, or by starving out the besieged, could obtain from them what they wanted. And then he thought of his preservers—those who had made him again a man, and an honest man, those to whom he owed all—murdered without pity, their works destroyed, their island turned into a pirates' den! He said to himself that he, Ayrton, was the principal cause of so many disasters, since his old companion, Bob Harvey, had but realised his own plans, and a feeling of horror took possession of him. Then he was seized with an irresistible desire to blow up the brig, and with her, all whom she had on board. He would perish in the explosion, but he would have done his duty.

Ayrton did not hesitate. To reach the powder-room, which is always situated in the after-part of a vessel, was easy. There would be no want of powder in a vessel which followed such a trade, and a spark would be enough to destroy it in an instant.

Ayrton stole carefully along the between-decks, strewn with numerous sleepers, overcome more by drunkenness than sleep. A lantern was lighted at the foot of the mainmast, round which was hung a gun-rack, furnished with weapons of all sorts.

Ayrton took a revolver from the rack, and assured himself that it was loaded and primed. Nothing more was needed to accomplish the work of destruction. He then glided towards the stern, so as to arrive under the brig's poop at the powder-magazine.

It was difficult to proceed along the dimly-lighted deck without stumbling over some half-sleeping convict, who retorted by oaths and kicks. Ayrton was, therefore, more than once obliged to halt. But at last he arrived at the partition dividing the after-cabin, and found the door opening into the magazine itself.

Ayrton, compelled to force it open, set to work. It was a difficult operation to perform without noise, for he had to break a padlock. But under his vigorous hand, the padlock broke, and the door was open.

At that moment a hand was laid on Ayrton's shoulder.

"What are you doing here?" asked a tall man, in a harsh voice, who, standing in the shadow, quickly threw the light of a lantern on Ayrton's face.

Ayrton drew back. In the rapid flash of the lantern, he had recognised his former accomplice, Bob Harvey, who could not have known him, as he must have thought Ayrton long since dead.

"What are you doing here?" again said Bob Harvey, seizing Ayrton by the waistband.

But Ayrton, without replying, wrenched himself from his grasp and attempted to rush into the magazine. A shot fired into the midst of the powder-casks, and all would be over!

"Help, lads!" shouted Bob Harvey.

At his shout two or three pirates awoke, jumped up, and, rushing on Ayrton, endeavoured to throw him down. He soon extricated himself from their grasp. He fired his revolver, and two of the convicts fell; but a blow from a knife which he could not ward off made a gash in his shoulder.

Ayrton perceived that he could no longer hope to carry out his project. Bob Harvey had reclosed the door of the powder-magazine, and a movement on the deck indicated a general awakening of the pirates. Ayrton must reserve himself to fight at the side of Cyrus Harding. There was nothing for him but flight!

But was flight still possible? It was doubtful, yet Ayrton resolved to dare everything in order to rejoin his companions.

Four barrels of the revolver were still undischarged. Two were fired—one, aimed at Bob Harvey, did not wound him, or at any rate only slightly; and Ayrton, profiting by the momentary retreat of his adversaries, rushed towards the companion-ladder to gain the deck. Passing before the lantern, he smashed it with a blow from the butt of his revolver. A profound darkness ensued, which favoured his flight. Two or three pirates, awakened by the noise, were descending the ladder at the same moment. A fifth shot from Ayrton laid one low, and the others drew back, not understanding what was going on. Ayrton was on deck in two bounds, and three seconds later, having discharged his last barrel in the face of a pirate who was about to seize him by the throat, he leapt over the bulwarks into the sea.

Ayrton had not made six strokes before shots were splashing around him like hail.

What were Pencroft's feelings, sheltered under a rock on the islet! what were those of Harding, the reporter, Herbert, and Neb, crouched in the Chimneys, when they heard the reports on board the brig! They rushed out onto the beach, and, their guns shouldered, they stood ready to repel any attack.

They had no doubt about it themselves! Ayrton, surprised by the pirates, had been murdered, and, perhaps, the wretches would profit by the night to make a descent on the island!

Half an hour was passed in terrible anxiety. The firing had ceased, and yet neither Ayrton nor Pencroft had reappeared. Was the islet invaded? Ought they not to fly to the help of Ayrton and Pencroft? But how? The tide being high at that time, rendered the channel impassable. The boat was not there! We may imagine the horrible anxiety which took possession of Harding and his companions!

At last, towards half-past twelve, a boat, carrying two men, touched the beach. It was Ayrton, slightly wounded in the shoulder, and Pencroft, safe and sound, whom their friends received with open arms. All immediately took refuge in the Chimneys. There Ayrton recounted all that had passed, even to his plan for blowing up the brig, which he had attempted to put into execution.

All hands were extended to Ayrton, who did not conceal from them that their situation was serious. The pirates had been alarmed. They knew that Lincoln Island was inhabited. They would land upon it in numbers and well-armed. They would respect nothing. Should the settlers fall into their hands, they must expect no mercy!

"Well, we shall know how to die!" said the reporter.

"Let us go in and watch," answered the engineer.

"Have we any chance of escape, captain?" asked the sailor.

"Yes, Pencroft."

"Hum! six against fifty!"

"Yes! six! without counting—"

"Who?" asked Pencroft.

Cyrus did not reply, but pointed upwards.

III

The Mist rises—The Engineer's Preparations—Three
Posts—Ayrton and Pencroft—The first Boat—Two
other Boats—On the Islet—Six Convicts land—The
Brig weighs Anchor—The Speedy's Guns—A desperate
Situation—Unexpected Catastrophe.

The night passed without incident. The colonists were on the *qui vive*, and did not leave their post at the Chimneys. The pirates, on their side, did not appear to have made any attempt to land. Since the last shots fired at Ayrton not a report, not even a sound, had betrayed the presence of the brig in the neighbourhood of the island. It might have been fancied that she had weighed anchor, thinking that she had to deal with her match, and had left the coast.

But it was no such thing, and when day began to dawn the settlers could see a confused mass through the morning mist. It was the *Speedy*.

"These, my friends," said the engineer, "are the arrangements which appear to me best to make before the fog completely clears away. It hides us from the eyes of the pirates, and we can act without attracting their attention. The most important thing is, that the convicts should believe that the inhabitants of the island are numerous, and consequently capable of resisting them. I therefore propose that we divide into three parties, the first of which shall be posted at the Chimneys, the second at the mouth of the Mercy. As to the third, I think it would be best to place it on the islet, so as to prevent, or at all events delay, any attempt at landing. We have the use of two rifles and four muskets. Each of us will be armed, and, as we are amply provided with powder and shot, we need not spare our fire. We have nothing to fear from the muskets, nor even from the guns of the brig. What can they do against these rocks? And, as we shall not fire from the windows of Granite House, the pirates will not think of causing irreparable damage by throwing shell against it. What is to be feared is, the necessity of meeting hand-to-hand, since the convicts have numbers on their side. We must, therefore, try to prevent them from landing, but without discovering ourselves. Therefore, do not economise the ammunition. Fire often, but with a sure aim. We have each eight or ten enemies to kill, and they must be killed!"

Cyrus Harding had clearly represented their situation, although he spoke in the calmest voice, as if it was a question of directing a piece of work, and not ordering a battle. His companions approved these arrangements without even uttering a word. There was nothing more to be done but for each to take his place before the fog should be completely dissipated. Neb and Pencroft immediately ascended to Granite House and brought back a sufficient quantity of ammunition. Gideon Spilett and Ayrton, both very good marksmen, were armed with the two rifles, which carried nearly a mile. The four other muskets were divided amongst Harding, Neb, Pencroft, and Herbert.

The posts were arranged in the following manner:—

Cyrus Harding and Herbert remained in ambush at the Chimneys, thus commanding the shore to the foot of Granite House.

Gideon Spilett and Neb crouched among the rocks at the mouth of the Mercy, from which the drawbridges had been raised, so as to prevent any one from crossing in a boat or landing on the opposite shore.

As to Ayrton and Pencroft, they shoved off in the boat, and prepared to cross the channel and to take up two separate stations on the islet. In this way, shots being fired from four different points at once, the convicts would be led to believe that the island was both largely peopled and strongly defended.

In the event of a landing being effected without their having been able to prevent it, and also if they saw that they were on the point of being cut off by the brig's boat, Ayrton and Pencroft were to return in their boat to the shore and proceed towards the threatened spot.

Before starting to occupy their posts, the colonists for the last time wrung each other's hands.

Pencroft succeeded in controlling himself sufficiently to suppress his emotion when he embraced Herbert, his boy! and then they separated.

In a few moments Harding and Herbert on one side, the reporter and Neb on the other, had disappeared behind the rocks, and five minutes later Ayrton and Pencroft, having without difficulty crossed the channel, disembarked on the islet and concealed themselves in the clefts of its eastern shore.

None of them could have been seen, for they themselves could scarcely distinguish the brig in the fog.

It was half-past six in the morning.

Soon the fog began to clear away, and the topmasts of the brig issued from the vapour. For some minutes great masses rolled over the surface of the sea, then a breeze sprang up, which rapidly dispelled the mist.

The *Speedy* now appeared in full view, with a spring on her cable, her head to the north, presenting her larboard side to the island. Just as Harding had calculated, she was not more than a mile and a quarter from the coast.

The sinister black flag floated from the peak.

The engineer, with his telescope, could see that the four guns on board were pointed at the island. They were evidently ready to fire at a moment's notice.

In the meanwhile the *Speedy* remained silent. About thirty pirates could be seen moving on the deck. A few were on the poop; two others posted in the shrouds, and armed with spy-glasses, were attentively surveying the island.

Certainly, Bob Harvey and his crew would not be able easily to give an account of what had happened during the night on board the brig. Had this half-naked man, who had forced the door of the powder-magazine, and with whom they had struggled, who had six times discharged his revolver at them, who had killed one and wounded two others, escaped their shot? Had he been able to swim to shore? Whence did he come? What had been his object? Had his design really been to blow up the brig, as Bob Harvey had thought? All this must be confused enough to the convicts' minds. But what they could no longer doubt was that the unknown island before which the *Speedy* had cast anchor was inhabited, and that there was, perhaps, a numerous colony ready to defend it. And yet no one was to be seen, neither on the shore, nor on the heights. The beach appeared to be absolutely deserted. At any rate, there was no trace of dwellings. Had the inhabitants fled into the interior? Thus probably the pirate captain reasoned, and doubtless, like a prudent man, he wished to reconnoitre the locality before he allowed his men to venture there.

During an hour and a half, no indication of attack or landing could be observed on board the brig. Evidently Bob Harvey was hesitating. Even with his strongest telescopes he could not have perceived one of the settlers crouched among the rocks. It was not even probable that his attention had been awakened by the screen of green branches and creepers hiding the windows of Granite House, and showing rather conspicuously on the bare rock. Indeed, how could he imagine that a dwelling was hollowed out, at that height, in the solid granite. From Claw Cape to the Mandible Capes, in all the extent of Union Bay, there was nothing to lead him to suppose that the island was or could be inhabited.

At eight o'clock, however, the colonists observed a movement on board the *Speedy*. A boat was lowered, and seven men jumped into her. They were armed with muskets: one took the yoke-lines, four others the oars, and the two others, kneeling in the bows, ready to fire, reconnoitred the island. Their object was no doubt to make an examination but not to land, for in the latter case they would have come in larger numbers. The pirates from their look-out could have seen that the coast was sheltered by an islet, separated from it by a channel half a mile in width. However, it was soon evident to Cyrus Harding, on observing the direction followed by the boat, that they would not attempt to penetrate into the channel, but would land on the islet.

Pencroft and Ayrton, each hidden in a narrow cleft of the rock, saw them coming directly towards them, and waited till they were within range.

The boat advanced with extreme caution. The oars only dipped into the water at long intervals. It could now be seen that one of the convicts held a lead-line in his hand, and that he wished to fathom the depth of the channel hollowed out by the current of the Mercy. This showed that it was Bob Harvey's intention to bring his brig as near as possible to the coast. About thirty pirates, scattered in the rigging, followed every movement of the boat, and took the bearings of certain landmarks which would allow them to approach without danger. The boat was not more than two cables-lengths off the islet when she stopped. The man at the tiller stood up and looked for the best place at which to land.

At that moment two shots were heard. Smoke curled up from among the rocks of the islet. The man at the helm and the man with the lead-line fell backwards into the boat. Ayrton's and Pencraft's balls had struck them both at the same moment.

Almost immediately a louder report was heard, a cloud of smoke issued from the brig's side, and a ball, striking the summit of the rock which sheltered Ayrton and Pencroft, made it fly in splinters, but the two marksmen remained unhurt.

Horrible imprecations burst from the boat, which immediately continued its way. The man who had been at the tiller was replaced by one of his comrades, and the oars were rapidly plunged into the water.

However, instead of returning on board as might have been expected, the boat coasted along the islet, so as to round its southern point. The pirates pulled vigorously at their oars that they might get out of range of the bullets.

They advanced to within five cables-lengths of that part of the shore terminated by Flotsam Point, and after having rounded it in a semicircular line, still protected by the brig's guns, they proceeded towards the mouth of the Mercy.

Their evident intention was to penetrate into the channel, and cut off the colonists posted on the islet, in such a way, that whatever their number might be, being placed between the fire from the boat and the fire from the brig, they would find themselves in a very disadvantageous position.

A quarter of an hour passed whilst the boat advanced in this direction. Absolute silence, perfect calm reigned in the air and on the water.

Pencroft and Ayrton, although they knew they ran the risk of being cut off, had not left their post, both that they did not wish to show themselves as yet to their assailants, and expose themselves to the *Speedy's* guns, and that they relied on Neb and Gideon Spilett, watching at the mouth of the river, and on Cyrus Harding and Herbert, in ambush among the rocks at the Chimneys.

Twenty minutes after the first shots were fired, the boat was less than two cables-lengths off the Mercy. As the tide was beginning to rise with its accustomed violence, caused by the narrowness of the straits, the pirates were drawn towards the river, and it was only by dint of hard rowing that they were able to keep in the middle of the channel. But, as they were passing within good range of the mouth of the Mercy, two balls saluted them, and two more of their number were laid in the bottom of the boat. Neb and Spilett had not missed their aim.

The brig immediately sent a second ball on the post betrayed by the smoke, but without any other result than that of splintering the rock.

The boat now contained only three able men. Carried on by the current, it shot through the channel with the rapidity of an arrow, passed before Harding and Herbert, who, not thinking it within range, withheld their fire, then, rounding the northern point of the islet with the two remaining oars, they pulled towards the brig.

Hitherto the settlers had nothing to complain of. Their adversaries had certainly had the worst of it. The latter already counted four men seriously wounded if not dead; they, on the contrary, unwounded, had not missed a shot. If the pirates continued to attack them in this way, if they renewed their attempt to land by means of a boat, they could be destroyed one by one.

It was now seen how advantageous the engineer's arrangements had been. The pirates would think that they had to deal with numerous and well-armed adversaries, whom they could not easily get the better of.

Half an hour passed before the boat, having to pull against the current, could get alongside the *Speedy*. Frightful cries were heard when they returned on board with the wounded, and two or three guns were fired with no result.

But now about a dozen other convicts, maddened with rage, and possibly by the effect of the evening's potations, threw themselves into the boat. A second boat was also lowered, in which eight men took their places, and whilst the first pulled straight for the islet, to dislodge the colonists from thence, the second manoeuvred so as to force the entrance of the Mercy.

The situation was evidently becoming very dangerous for Pencroft and Ayrton, and they saw that they must regain the mainland.

However, they waited till the first boat was within range, when two well-directed balls threw its crew into disorder. Then, Pencroft and Ayrton, abandoning their posts, under fire from the dozen muskets, ran across the islet at full speed, jumped into their boat, crossed the channel at the moment the second boat reached the southern end, and ran to hide themselves in the Chimneys.

They had scarcely rejoined Cyrus Harding and Herbert, before the islet was overrun with pirates in every direction. Almost at the same moment, fresh reports resounded from the Mercy station, to which the second boat was rapidly approaching. Two, out of the eight men who manned her, were mortally wounded by Gideon Spilett and Neb, and the boat herself, carried irresistibly onto the reefs, was stove in at the mouth of the Mercy. But the six survivors, holding their muskets above their heads to preserve them from contact with the water, managed to land on the right bank of the river. Then, finding they were exposed to the fire of the ambush there, they fled in the direction of Flotsam Point, out of range of the balls.

The actual situation was this: on the islet were a dozen convicts, of whom some were no doubt wounded, but who had still a boat at their disposal; on the island were six, but who could not by any possibility reach Granite House, as they could not cross the river, all the bridges being raised.

"Hallo," exclaimed Pencroft as he rushed into the Chimneys, "hallo, captain! What do you think of it, now?"

"I think," answered the engineer, "that the combat will now take a new form, for it cannot be supposed that the convicts will be so foolish as to remain in a position so unfavourable for them!"

"They won't cross the channel," said the sailor. "Ayrton and Mr. Spilett's rifles are there to prevent them. You know that they carry more than a mile!"

"No doubt," replied Herbert; "but what can two rifles do against the brig's guns?"

"Well, the brig isn't in the channel yet, I fancy!" said Pencroft.

"But suppose she does come there?" said Harding.

"That's impossible, for she would risk running aground and being lost!"

"It is possible," said Ayrton. "The convicts might profit by the high tide to enter the channel, with the risk of grounding at low tide, it is true; but then, under the fire from her guns, our posts would be no longer tenable."

"Confound them!" exclaimed Pencroft. "It really seems as if the blackguards were preparing to weigh anchor."

"Perhaps we shall be obliged to take refuge in Granite House!" observed Herbert.

"We must wait!" answered Cyrus Harding.

"But Mr. Spilett and Neb?" said Pencroft.

"They will know when it is best to rejoin us. Be ready, Ayrton. It is yours and Spilett's rifles which must speak now."

It was only too true. The *Speedy* was beginning to weigh her anchor, and her intention was evidently to approach the islet. The tide would be rising for an hour and a half, and the ebb current being already weakened, it would be easy for the brig to advance. But as to entering the channel, Pencroft, contrary to Ayrton's opinion, could not believe that she would dare to attempt it.

In the meanwhile, the pirates who occupied the islet had gradually advanced to the opposite shore, and were now only separated from the mainland by the channel.

Being armed with muskets alone, they could do no harm to the settlers, in ambush at the Chimneys and the mouth of the Mercy; but, not knowing the latter to be supplied with long range rifles, they on their side did not believe themselves to be exposed. Quite uncovered, therefore, they surveyed the islet, and examined the shore.

Their illusion was of short duration. Ayrton's and Gideon Spilett's rifles then spoke, and no doubt imparted some very disagreeable intelligence to two of the convicts, for they fell backwards.

Then there was a general helter-skelter. The ten others, not even stopping to pick up their dead or wounded companions, fled to the other side of the islet, tumbled into the boat which had brought them, and pulled away with all their strength.

"Eight less!" exclaimed Pencroft. "Really, one would have thought that Mr. Spilett and Ayrton had given the word to fire together!"

"Gentlemen," said Ayrton, as he reloaded his gun, "this is becoming more serious. The brig is making sail!"

"The anchor is weighed!" exclaimed Pencroft.

"Yes; and she is already moving."

In fact, they could distinctly hear the creaking of the windlass. The *Speedy* was at first held by her anchor; then, when that had been raised, she began to drift towards the shore. The wind was blowing from the sea; the jib and the fore-topsail were hoisted, and the vessel gradually approached the island.

From the two posts of the Mercy and the Chimneys they watched her without giving a sign of life; but not without some emotion. What could be more terrible for the colonists than to be exposed, at a short distance, to the brig's guns, without being able to reply with any effect? How could they then prevent the pirates from landing?

Cyrus Harding felt this strongly, and he asked himself what it would be possible to do. Before long, he would be called upon for his determination. But what was it to be? To shut themselves up in Granite House, to be besieged there, to remain there for weeks, for months even, since they had an abundance of provisions? So far good! But after that? The pirates would not the less be masters of the island, which they would ravage at their pleasure, and in time they would end by having their revenge on the prisoners in Granite House.

However, one chance yet remained; it was that Bob Harvey, after all, would not venture his ship into the channel, and that he would keep outside the islet. He would be still separated from the coast by half a mile, and at that distance his shot could not be very destructive.

"Never!" repeated Pencroft, "Bob Harvey will never, if he is a good seaman, enter that channel! He knows well that it would risk the brig, if the sea got up ever so little! And what would become of him without his vessel?"

In the meanwhile the brig approached the islet, and it could be seen that she was endeavouring to make the lower end. The breeze was light, and as the current had then lost much of its force, Bob Harvey had absolute command over his vessel.

The route previously followed by the boats had allowed her to reconnoitre the channel, and she boldly entered it.

The pirate's design was now only too evident: he wished to bring her broadside to bear on the Chimneys and from there to reply with shell and ball to the shot which had till then decimated her crew.

Soon the *Speedy* reached the point of the islet; she rounded it with ease; the mainsail was braced up, and the brig hugging the wind, stood across the mouth of the Mercy.

"The scoundrels! they are coming!" said Pencroft.

At that moment, Cyrus Harding, Ayrton, the sailor, and Herbert, were rejoined by Neb and Gideon Spilett.

The reporter and his companion had judged it best to abandon the post at the Mercy, from which they could do nothing against the ship, and they had acted wisely. It was better that the colonists should be together at the moment when they were about to engage in a decisive action. Gideon Spilett and Neb had arrived by dodging behind the rocks, though not without attracting a shower of bullets, which had not, however, reached them.

"Spilett! Neb!" cried the engineer, "you are not wounded?"

"No," answered the reporter; "a few bruises only from the ricochet! But that cursed brig has entered the channel!"

"Yes," replied Pencroft, "and in ten minutes she will have anchored before Granite House!"

"Have you formed any plan, Cyrus?" asked the reporter.

"We must take refuge in Granite House whilst there is still time, and the convicts cannot see us."

"That is my opinion, too," replied Gideon Spilett; "but once shut up—"

"We must be guided by circumstances," said the engineer.

"Let us be off, then, and make haste!" said the reporter.

"Would you not wish, captain, that Ayrton and I should remain here?" asked the sailor.

"What would be the use of that, Pencroft?" replied Harding. "No. We will not separate!"

There was not a moment to be lost. The colonists left the Chimneys. A bend of the cliff prevented them from being seen by those in the brig; but two or three reports, and the crash of bullets on the rock, told them that the *Speedy* was at no great distance.

To spring into the lift, hoist themselves up to the door of Granite House, where Top and Jup had been shut up since the evening before, to rush into the large room, was the work of a minute only.

It was quite time, for the settlers, through the branches, could see the *Speedy*, surrounded with smoke, gliding up the channel. The firing was incessant, and shot from the four guns struck blindly, both on the Mercy post, although it was not occupied, and on the Chimneys. The rocks were splintered, and cheers accompanied each discharge. However, they were hoping that Granite House would be spared, thanks to Harding's precaution of concealing the windows, when a shot, piercing the door, penetrated into the passage.

"We are discovered!" exclaimed Pencroft.

The colonists had not, perhaps, been seen; but it was certain that Bob Harvey had thought proper to send a ball through the suspected foliage which concealed that part of the cliff. Soon he redoubled his attack, when another ball having torn away the leafy screen, disclosed a gaping aperture in the granite.

The colonists' situation was desperate. Their retreat was discovered. They could not oppose any obstacle to these missiles, nor protect the stone, which flew in splinters around them. There was nothing to be done but to take refuge in the upper passage of Granite House, and leave their dwelling to be devastated, when a deep roar was heard, followed by frightful cries!

Cyrus Harding and his companions rushed to one of the windows—

The brig, irresistibly raised on a sort of water-spout, had just split in two, and in less than ten seconds she was swallowed up with all her criminal crew!

IV

S he has blown up!" cried Herbert.

"Yes! blown up, just as if Ayrton had set fire to the powder!" returned Pencroft, throwing himself into the lift together with Neb and the lad.

"But what has happened?" asked Gideon Spilett, quite stunned by this unexpected catastrophe.

"Oh! this time, we shall know," answered the engineer quickly.

"What shall we know?—"

"Later! later! Come, Spilett. The main point is that these pirates have been exterminated!"

And Cyrus Harding, hurrying away the reporter and Ayrton, joined Pencroft, Neb, and Herbert on the beach.

Nothing could be seen of the brig, not even her masts. After having been raised by the water-spout, she had fallen on her side, and had sunk in that position, doubtless in consequence of some enormous leak. But as in that place the channel was not more than twenty feet in depth, it was certain that the sides of the submerged brig would reappear at low-water.

A few things from the wreck floated on the surface of the water. A raft could be seen consisting of spare spars, coops of poultry with their occupants still living, boxes and barrels, which gradually came to the surface, after having escaped through the hatchways, but no pieces of the wreck appeared, neither planks from the deck, nor timber from the hull,—which rendered the sudden disappearance of the *Speedy* perfectly inexplicable.

However, the two masts, which had been broken and escaped from the shrouds and stays, came up, with their sails, some furled and the others spread. But it was not necessary to wait for the tide to bring up these riches, and Ayrton and Pencroft, jumped into the boat with the intention of towing the pieces of wreck either to the beach or to the islet. But just as they were shoving off an observation from Gideon Spilett arrested them.

"What about those six convicts who disembarked on the right bank of the Mercy?" said he.

In fact, it would not do to forget that the six men whose boat had gone to pieces on the rocks, had landed at Flotsam Point.

They looked in that direction. None of the fugitives were visible. It was probable that, having seen their vessel engulfed in the channel, they had fled into the interior of the island.

"We will deal with them later," said Harding. "As they are armed, they will still be dangerous; but as it is six against six, the chances are equal. To the most pressing business first."

Ayrton and Pencroft pulled vigorously towards the wreck.

The sea was calm and the tide very high, as there had been a new moon but two days before. A whole hour at least would elapse before the hull of the brig could emerge from the water of the channel.

Ayrton and Pencroft were able to fasten the masts and spars by means of ropes, the ends of which were carried to the beach. There, by the united efforts of the settlers the pieces of wreck were hauled up. Then the boat picked up all that was floating, coops, barrels, and boxes, which were immediately carried to the Chimneys.

Several bodies floated also. Amongst them, Ayrton recognised that of Bob Harvey, which he pointed out to his companion, saying with some emotion—

"That is what I have been, Pencroft."

"But what you are no longer, brave Ayrton!" returned the sailor warmly.

It was singular enough that so few bodies floated. Only five or six were counted, which were already being carried by the current towards the open sea. Very probably the convicts had not had time to escape, and the ship lying over on her side, the greater number of them had remained below. Now the current, by carrying the bodies of these miserable men out to sea, would spare the colonists the sad task of burying them in some corner of their island.

For two hours, Cyrus Harding and his companions were solely occupied in hauling up the spars onto the sand, and then in spreading the sails, which were perfectly uninjured, to dry. They spoke little, for they were absorbed in their work, but what thoughts occupied their minds!

The possession of this brig, or rather all that she contained, was a perfect mine of wealth. In fact, a ship is like a little world in miniature, and the stores of the colony would be increased by a large number of useful articles. It would be, on a large scale, equivalent to the chest found at Flotsam Point.

"And besides," thought Pencroft, "why should it be impossible to refloat the brig? If she has only a leak, that may be stopped up; a vessel from three to four hundred tons, why she is a regular ship compared to our *Bonadventure*! And we could go a long distance in her! We could go anywhere we liked! Captain Harding, Ayrton and I must examine her! She would be well worth the trouble!"

In fact, if the brig was still fit to navigate, the colonists' chances of returning to their native land was singularly increased. But, to decide this important question, it was necessary to wait until the tide was quite low, so that every part of the brig's hull might be examined.

When their treasures had been safely conveyed on shore, Harding and his companions agreed to devote some minutes to breakfast. They were almost famished: fortunately, the larder was not far off, and Neb was noted for being an expeditious cook. They breakfasted, therefore, near the Chimneys, and during their repast, as may be supposed, nothing was talked of but the unexpected event which had so miraculously saved the colony.

"Miraculous is the word," repeated Pencroft, "for it must be acknowledged that those rascals blew up just at the right moment! Granite House was beginning to be uncomfortable as a habitation!"

"And can you guess, Pencroft," asked the reporter, "how it happened, or what can have occasioned the explosion?"

"Oh! Mr. Spilett, nothing is more simple," answered Pencroft. "A convict vessel is not disciplined like a man-of-war! Convicts are not sailors. Of course the powder-magazine was open, and as they were firing incessantly, some careless or clumsy fellow just blew up the vessel!"

"Captain Harding," said Herbert, "what astonishes me is that the explosion has not produced more effect. The report was not loud, and besides there are so few planks and timbers torn out. It seems as if the ship had rather foundered than blown up."

"Does that astonish you, my boy?" asked the engineer.

"Yes, captain."

"And it astonishes me also Herbert," replied he, "but when we visit the hull of the brig, we shall no doubt find the explanation of the matter."

"Why, captain," said Pencroft, "you don't suppose that the *Speedy* simply foundered like a ship which has struck on a rock?"

"Why not," observed Neb, "if there are rocks in the channel?"

"Nonsense, Neb," answered Pencroft, "you did not look at the right moment. An instant before she sank, the brig, as I saw perfectly well, rose on an enormous wave, and fell back on her larboard side. Now, if she had only struck, she would have sunk quietly and gone to the bottom like an honest vessel."

"It was just because she was not an honest vessel!" returned Neb.

"Well, we shall soon see, Pencroft," said the engineer.

"We shall soon see," rejoined the sailor, "but I would wager my head there are no rocks in the channel. Look here, captain, to speak candidly, do you mean to say that there is anything marvellous in the occurrence?"

Cyrus Harding did not answer.

"At any rate," said Gideon Spilett, "whether rock or explosion, you will agree, Pencroft, that it occurred just in the nick of time!"

"Yes! yes!" replied the sailor, "but that is not the question. I ask Captain Harding if he sees anything supernatural in all this."

"I cannot say, Pencroft," said the engineer. "That is all the answer I can make."

A reply which did not satisfy Pencroft at all. He stuck to "an explosion," and did not wish to give it up. He would never consent to admit that in that channel, with its fine sandy bed, just like the beach, which he had often crossed at low-water, there could be an unknown rock.

And besides, at the time the brig foundered, it was high-water, that is to say, there was enough water to carry the vessel clear over any rocks which would not be uncovered at low tide. Therefore, there could not have been a collision. Therefore, the vessel had not struck. Therefore, she had blown up.

And it must be confessed that the sailor's arguments were not without reason.

Towards half-past one, the colonists embarked in the boat to visit the wreck. It was to be regretted that the brig's two boats had not been saved; but one, as has been said, had gone to pieces at the mouth of the Mercy, and was absolutely useless; the other had disappeared when the brig went down, and had not again been seen, having doubtless been crushed.

The hull of the *Speedy* was just beginning to issue from the water. The brig was lying right over on her side, for her masts being broken, pressed down by the weight of the ballast displaced by the shock, the keel was visible along her whole length. She had been regularly turned over by the inexplicable but frightful submarine action, which had been at the same time manifested by an enormous water-spout.

The settlers rowed round the hull, and, in proportion as the tide went down, they could ascertain, if not the cause which had occasioned the catastrophe, at least the effect produced.

Towards the bows, on both sides of the keel, seven or eight feet from the beginning of the stem, the sides of the brig were frightfully torn. Over a length of at least twenty feet there opened two large leaks, which it would be impossible to stop up. Not only had the copper sheathing and the planks disappeared, reduced, no doubt, to powder, but also the ribs, the iron bolts, and tree-nails which united them. From the entire length of the hull to the stern the false keel had been separated with unaccountable violence, and the keel itself, torn from the carline in several places, was split in all its length.

"I've a notion!" exclaimed Pencroft, "that this vessel will be difficult to get afloat again."

"It will be impossible," said Ayrton.

"At any rate," observed Gideon Spilett to the sailor, "the explosion, if there has been one, has produced singular effects! It has split the lower part of the hull, instead of blowing up the deck and topsides! These great rents appear rather to have been made by a rock than by the explosion of a powder-magazine."

"There is not a rock in the channel!" answered the sailor. "I will admit anything you like, except the rock."

"Let us try to penetrate into the interior of the brig," said the engineer; "perhaps we shall then know what to think of the cause of her destruction."

This was the best thing to be done, and it was agreed, besides, to take an inventory of all the treasures on board, and to arrange for their preservation.

Access to the interior of the brig was now easy. The tide was still going down, and the deck was practicable. The ballast, composed of heavy masses of iron, had broken through in several places. The noise of the sea could be heard as it rushed out at the holes in the hull.

Cyrus Harding and his companions, hatchets in hand, advanced along the shattered deck. Cases of all sorts encumbered it, and, as they had been but a very short time in the water, their contents were perhaps uninjured.

They then busied themselves in placing all this cargo in safety. The water would not return for several hours, and these hours must be employed in the most profitable way. Ayrton and Pencroft had, at the entrance made in the hull, discovered tackle, which would serve to hoist up the barrels and chests. The boat received them and transported them to the shore. They took the articles as they came, intending to sort them afterwards.

At any rate, the settlers saw at once, with extreme satisfaction, that the brig possessed a very varied cargo—an assortment of all sorts of articles, utensils, manufactured goods, and tools—such as the ships which make the great coasting-trade of Polynesia are usually laden with. It was probable that they would find a little of everything, and they agreed that it was exactly what was necessary for the colony of Lincoln Island.

However—and Cyrus Harding observed it in silent astonishment—not only, as has been said, had the hull of the brig enormously suffered from the shock, whatever it was, that had occasioned the catastrophe, but the interior arrangements had been destroyed, especially towards the bows. Partitions and staunchions were smashed, as if some tremendous shell had burst in the interior of the brig. The colonists could easily go fore and aft, after having removed the cases as they were extricated. They were not heavy bales, which would have been difficult to remove, but simple packages, of which the stowage, besides, was no longer recognisable.

The colonists then reached the stern of the brig—the part formerly surmounted by the poop. It was there that, following Ayrton's directions, they must look for the powder-magazine. Cyrus Harding thought that it had not exploded; that it was possible some barrels might be saved, and that the powder, which is usually enclosed in metal coverings, might not have suffered from contact with the water.

This, in fact, was just what had happened. They extricated from amongst a large number of shot twenty barrels, the insides of which were lined with copper. Pencroft was convinced by the evidence of his own eyes that the destruction of the *Speedy* could not be attributed to an explosion. That part of the hull in which the magazine was situated was, moreover, that which had suffered least.

"It may be so," said the obstinate sailor; "but as to a rock, there is not one in the channel!"

"Then, how did it happen?" asked Herbert.

"I don't know," answered Pencroft, "Captain Harding doesn't know, and nobody knows or ever will know!"

Several hours had passed during these researches, and the tide began to flow. Work must be suspended for the present. There was no fear of the brig being carried away by the sea, for she was already fixed as firmly as if moored by her anchors.

They could therefore, without inconvenience, wait until the next day to resume operations; but, as to the vessel herself, she was doomed, and it would be best to hasten to save the remains of her hull, as she would not be long in disappearing in the quicksands of the channel.

It was now five o'clock in the evening. It had been a hard day's work for the men. They ate with good appetite, and, notwithstanding their fatigue, they could not resist, after dinner, their desire of inspecting the cases which composed the cargo of the *Speedy*.

Most of them contained clothes, which, as may be believed, were well received. There were enough to clothe a whole colony—linen for every one's use, shoes for every one's feet.

"We are too rich!" exclaimed Pencroft. "But what are we going to do with all this?"

And every moment burst forth the hurrahs of the delighted sailor when he caught sight of the barrels of gunpowder, fire-arms and side-arms, balls of cotton, implements of husbandry, carpenter's, joiner's, and blacksmith's tools, and boxes of all kinds of seeds, not in the least injured by their short sojourn in the water. Ah, two years before, how these things would have been prized! And now, even although the industrious colonists had provided themselves with tools, these treasures would find their use.

There was no want of space in the store-rooms of Granite House, but that daytime would not allow them to stow away the whole. It would not do also to forget that the six survivors of the *Speedy's* crew had landed on the island, for they were in all probability scoundrels of the deepest dye, and it was necessary that the colonists should be on their guard against them. Although the bridges over the Mercy were raised, the convicts would not be stopped by a river or a stream, and, rendered desperate, these wretches would be capable of anything.

They would see later what plan it would be best to follow; but in the meantime it was necessary to mount guard over cases and packages heaped up near the Chimneys, and thus the settlers employed themselves in turn during the night.

The morning came, however, without the convicts having attempted any attack. Master Jup and Top, on guard at the foot of Granite House, would have quickly given the alarm. The three following days—the 19th, 20th, and 21st of October—were employed in saving everything of value, or of any use whatever, either from the cargo or rigging of the brig. At low tide they overhauled the hold—at high tide they stowed away the rescued articles. A great part of the copper sheathing had been torn from the hull, which every day sank lower. But before the sand had swallowed the heavy things which had fallen through the bottom, Ayrton and Pencroft, diving to the bed of the channel, recovered the chains and anchors of the brig, the iron of her ballast, and even four guns, which, floated by means of empty casks, were brought to shore.

It may be seen that the arsenal of the colony had gained by the wreck, as well as the store-rooms of Granite House. Pencroft, always enthusiastic in his projects, already spoke of constructing a battery to command the channel and the mouth of the river. With four guns, he engaged to prevent any fleet, "however powerful it might be," from venturing into the waters of Lincoln Island!

In the meantime, when nothing remained of the brig but a useless hulk, bad weather came on, which soon finished her. Cyrus Harding had intended to blow her up, so as to collect the remains on the shore, but a strong gale from the north-east and a heavy sea compelled him to economise his powder.

In fact, on the night of the 23rd, the hull entirely broke up, and some of the wreck was cast up on the beach.

As to the papers on board, it is useless to say that, although he carefully searched the lockers of the poop, Harding did not discover any trace of them. The pirates had evidently destroyed everything that concerned either the captain or the owners of the *Speedy*, and, as the name of her port was not painted on her counter, there was nothing which would tell them her nationality. However, by the shape of her boats Ayrton and Pencroft believed that the brig was of English build.

A week after the catastrophe—or, rather, after the fortunate, though inexplicable, event to which the colony owed its preservation—nothing more could be seen of the vessel, even at low tide. The wreck had disappeared, and Granite House was enriched by nearly all it had contained.

However, the mystery which enveloped its strange destruction would doubtless never have been cleared away if, on the 30th of November, Neb, strolling on the beach, had not found a piece of a thick iron cylinder, bearing traces of explosion. The edges of this cylinder were twisted and broken, as if they had been subjected to the action of some explosive substance.

Neb brought this piece of metal to his master, who was then occupied with his companions in the workshop of the Chimneys.

Cyrus Harding examined the cylinder attentively, then, turning to Pencroft—

"You persist, my friend," said he, "in maintaining that the *Speedy* was not lost in consequence of a collision?"

"Yes, captain," answered the sailor. "You know as well as I do that there are no rocks in the channel."

"But suppose she had run against this piece of iron?" said the engineer, showing the broken cylinder.

"What, that bit of pipe!" exclaimed Pencroft in a tone of perfect incredulity.

"My friends," resumed Harding, "you remember that before she foundered the brig rose on the summit of a regular water-spout?"

"Yes, captain," replied Herbert.

"Well, would you like to know what occasioned that water-spout? It was this," said the engineer, holding up the broken tube.

"That?" returned Pencroft.

"Yes! This cylinder is all that remains of a torpedo!"

"A torpedo!" exclaimed the engineer's companions.

"And who put the torpedo there?" demanded Pencroft, who did not like to yield.

"All that I can tell you is, that it was not I," answered Cyrus Harding; "but it was there, and you have been able to judge of its incomparable power!"

V

The Engineer's Declaration—Pencroft's grand
Hypothesis—An aerial Battery—The four Cannons—
The surviving Convicts—Ayrton's Hesitation—Cyrus
Harding's generous Sentiments—Pencroft's Regret.

So, then, all was explained by the submarine explosion of this torpedo. Cyrus Harding could not be mistaken, as, during the war of the Union, he had had occasion to try these terrible engines of destruction. It was under the action of this cylinder, charged with some explosive substance, nitro-glycerine, picrate, or some other material of the same nature, that the water of the channel had been raised like a dome, the bottom of the brig crushed in, and she had sunk instantly, the damage done to her hull being so considerable that it was impossible to refloat her. The *Speedy* had not been able to withstand a torpedo that would have destroyed an ironclad as easily as a fishing-boat!

Yes! all was explained, everything—except the presence of the torpedo in the waters of the channel!

"My friends, then," said Cyrus Harding, "we can no longer be in doubt as to the presence of a mysterious being, a castaway like us, perhaps, abandoned on our island, and I say this in order that Ayrton may be acquainted with all the strange events which have occurred during these two years. Who this beneficent stranger is, whose intervention has, so fortunately for us, been manifested on many occasions, I cannot imagine. What his object can be in acting thus, in concealing himself after rendering us so many services, I cannot understand. But his services are not the less real, and are of such a nature that only a man possessed of prodigious power, could render them. Ayrton is indebted to him as much as we are, for, if it was the stranger who saved me from the waves after the fall from the balloon, evidently it was he who wrote the document, who placed the bottle in the channel, and who has made known to us the situation of our companion. I will add that it was he who guided that chest, provided with everything we wanted, and stranded it on Flotsam Point; that it was he who lighted that fire on the heights of the island, which permitted you to land; that it was he who fired that bullet found in the body of the peccary; that it was he who immersed that torpedo in the channel, which destroyed the brig; in a word, that all those inexplicable events, for which we could not assign a reason, are due to this mysterious being. Therefore, whoever he may be, whether shipwrecked, or exiled on our island, we shall be ungrateful, if we think ourselves freed from gratitude towards him. We have contracted a debt, and I hope that we shall one day pay it."

"You are right in speaking thus, my dear Cyrus," replied Gideon Spilett. "Yes, there is an almost all-powerful being, hidden in some part of the island, and whose influence has been singularly useful to our colony. I will add that the unknown appears to possess means of action which border on the supernatural if, in the events of practical life, the supernatural were recognisable. Is it he who is in secret communication with us by the well in Granite House, and has he thus a knowledge of all our plans? Was it he who threw us that bottle, when the vessel made her first cruise? Was it he who threw Top out of the lake, and killed the dugong? Was it he, who as everything leads us to believe, saved you from the waves, and that under circumstances in which any one else would not have been able to act? If it was he, he possesses a power which renders him master of the elements."

The reporter's reasoning was just, and every one felt it to be so.

"Yes," rejoined Cyrus Harding, "if the intervention of a human being is not more questionable for us, I agree that he has at his disposal means of action beyond those possessed by humanity. There is a mystery still, but if we discover the man, the mystery will be discovered also. The question, then, is, ought we to respect the *incognito* of this generous being, or ought we to do everything to find him out? What is your opinion on the matter?"

"My opinion," said Pencroft, "is that, whoever he may be, he is a brave man, and he has my esteem!"

"Be it so," answered Harding, "but that is not an answer, Pencroft."

"Master," then said Neb, "my idea is, that we may search as long as we like for this gentleman whom you are talking about, but that we shall not discover him till he pleases."

"That's not bad, what you say, Neb," observed Pencroft.

"I am of Neb's opinion," said Gideon Spilett, "but that is no reason for not attempting the adventure. Whether we find this mysterious being or not, we shall at least have fulfilled our duty towards him."

"And you, my boy, give us your opinion," said the engineer, turning to Herbert.

"Oh," cried Herbert, his countenance full of animation, "how I should like to thank him, he who saved you first, and who has now saved us!"

"Of course, my boy," replied Pencroft, "so would I and all of us. I am not inquisitive, but I would give one of my eyes to see this individual face to face! It seems to me that he must be handsome, tall, strong, with a splendid beard, radiant hair, and that he must be seated on the clouds, a great ball in his hands!"

"But, Pencroft," answered Spilett, "you are describing a picture of the Creator."

"Possibly, Mr. Spilett," replied the sailor, "but that is how I imagine him!"

"And you, Ayrton?" asked the engineer.

"Captain Harding," replied Ayrton, "I can give you no better advice in this matter. Whatever you do will be best, when you wish me to join you in your researches, I am ready to follow you."

"I thank you, Ayrton," answered Cyrus Harding, "but I should like a more direct answer to the question I put to you. You are our companion; you have already endangered your life several times for us, and you, as well as the rest, ought to be consulted in the matter of any important decision. Speak, therefore."

"Captain Harding," replied Ayrton, "I think that we ought to do everything to discover this unknown benefactor. Perhaps he is alone. Perhaps he is suffering. Perhaps he has a life to be renewed. I, too, as you said, have a debt of gratitude to pay him. It was he, it could be only he who must have come to Tabor Island, who found there the wretch you knew, and who made known to you that there was an unfortunate man there to be saved! Therefore it is, thanks to him, that I have become a man again. No, I will never forget him!"

"That is settled, then," said Cyrus Harding. "We will begin our researches as soon as possible. We will not leave a corner of the island unexplored. We will search into its most secret recesses, and will hope that our unknown friend will pardon us in consideration of our intentions!"

For several days the colonists were actively employed in haymaking and harvest. Before putting their project of exploring the yet unknown parts of the island into execution, they wished to get all possible work finished. It was also the time for collecting the various vegetables from the Tabor Island plants. All was stowed away, and happily there was no want of room in Granite House, in which they might have housed all the treasures of the island. The products of the colony were there, methodically arranged, and in a safe place, as may be believed, sheltered as much from animals as from man.

There was no fear of damp in the middle of that thick mass of granite. Many natural excavations situated in the upper passage were enlarged either by pick-axe or mine, and Granite House thus became a general warehouse, containing all the provisions, arms, tools, and spare utensils—in a word, all the stores of the colony.

As to the guns obtained from the brig, they were pretty pieces of ordnance, which, at Pencroft's entreaty, were hoisted by means of tackle and pulleys, right up into Granite House; embrasures were made between the windows, and the shining muzzles of the guns could soon be seen through the granite cliff. From this height they commanded all Union Bay. It was like a little Gibraltar, and any vessel anchored off the islet would inevitably be exposed to the fire of this aerial battery.

"Captain," said Pencroft one day, it was the 8th of November, "now that our fortifications are finished, it would be a good thing if we tried the range of our guns."

"Do you think that is useful?" asked the engineer.

"It is more than useful, it is necessary! Without that how are we to know to what distance we can send one of those pretty shot with which we are provided?"

"Try them, Pencroft," replied the engineer. "However, I think that in making the experiment, we ought to employ, not the ordinary powder, the supply of which, I think, should remain untouched, but the pyroxile which will never fail us."

"Can the cannon support the shock of the pyroxile?" asked the reporter, who was not less anxious than Pencroft to try the artillery of Granite House.

"I believe so. However," added the engineer, "we will be prudent."

The engineer was right in thinking that the guns were of excellent make. Made of forged steel, and breech-loaders, they ought consequently to be able to bear a considerable charge, and also have an enormous range. In fact, as regards practical effect, the transit described by the ball ought to be as extended as possible, and this tension could only be obtained under the condition that the projectile should be impelled with a very great initial velocity.

"Now," said Harding to his companions, "the initial velocity is in proportion to the quantity of powder used. In the fabrication of these pieces, everything depends on employing a metal with the highest possible power of resistance, and steel is incontestably that metal of all others which resists the best. I have, therefore, reason to believe that our guns will bear without risk the expansion of the pyroxile gas, and will give excellent results."

"We shall be a great deal more certain of that when we have tried them!" answered Pencroft.

It is unnecessary to say that the four cannons were in perfect order. Since they had been taken from the water, the sailor had bestowed great care upon them. How many hours he had spent, in rubbing, greasing, and polishing them, and in cleaning the mechanism! And now the pieces were as brilliant as if they had been on board a frigate of the United States' Navy.

On this day, therefore, in presence of all the members of the colony, including Master Jup and Top, the four cannon were successively tried. They were charged with pyroxile, taking into consideration its explosive power, which, as has been said, is four times that of ordinary powder: the projectile to be fired was cylindro-conic.

Pencroft, holding the end of the quick-match, stood ready to fire.

At Harding's signal, he fired. The shot, passing over the islet, fell into the sea at a distance which could not be calculated with exactitude.

The second gun was pointed at the rocks at the end of Flotsam Point, and the shot, striking a sharp rock nearly three miles from Granite House, made it fly into splinters. It was Herbert who had pointed this gun and fired it, and very proud he was of his first shot. Pencroft only was prouder than he! Such a shot, the honour of which belonged to his dear boy.

The third shot, aimed this time at the downs forming the upper side of Union Bay, struck the sand at a distance of four miles, then having ricocheted, was lost in the sea in a cloud of spray.

For the fourth piece Cyrus Harding slightly increased the charge, so as to try its extreme range. Then, all standing aside for fear of its bursting, the match was lighted by means of a long cord.

A tremendous report was heard, but the piece had held good, and the colonists rushing to the windows, saw the shot graze the rocks of Mandible Cape, nearly five miles from Granite House, and disappear in Shark Gulf.

"Well, captain," exclaimed Pencroft, whose cheers might have rivalled the reports themselves, "what do you say of our battery? All the pirates in the Pacific have only to present themselves before Granite House! Not one can land there now without our permission!"

"Believe me, Pencroft," replied the engineer, "it would be better not to have to make the experiment."

"Well," said the sailor, "what ought to be done with regard to those six villains who are roaming about the island? Are we to leave them to overrun our forests, our fields, our plantations. These pirates are regular jaguars, and it seems to me we ought not to hesitate to treat them as such! What do you think, Ayrton?" added Pencroft, turning to his companion.

Ayrton hesitated at first to reply, and Cyrus Harding regretted that Pencroft had so thoughtlessly put this question. And he was much moved when Ayrton replied in a humble tone—

"I have been one of those jaguars, Mr. Pencroft. I have no right to speak."

And with a slow step he walked away.

Pencroft understood.

"What a brute I am!" he exclaimed. "Poor Ayrton! He has as much right to speak here as any one!"

"Yes," said Gideon Spilett, "but his reserve does him honour, and it is right to respect the feeling which he has about his sad past."

"Certainly, Mr. Spilett," answered the sailor, "and there is no fear of my doing so again. I would rather bite my tongue off than cause Ayrton any pain! But to return to the question. It seems to me that these ruffians have no right to any pity, and that we ought to rid the island of them as soon as possible."

"Is that your opinion, Pencroft?" asked the engineer.

"Quite my opinion."

"And before hunting them mercilessly, you would not wait until they had committed some fresh act of hostility against us?"

"Isn't what they have done already enough?" asked Pencroft, who did not understand these scruples.

"They may adopt other sentiments!" said Harding, "and perhaps repent."

"They repent!" exclaimed the sailor, shrugging his shoulders.

"Pencroft, think of Ayrton!" said Herbert, taking the sailor's hand. "He became an honest man again!"

Pencroft looked at his companions one after the other. He had never thought of his proposal being met with any objection. His rough nature could not allow that they ought to come to terms with the rascals who had landed on the island with Bob Harvey's accomplices, the murderers of the crew of the *Speedy*; and he looked upon them as wild beasts which ought to be destroyed without delay and without remorse.

"Come!" said he. "Everybody is against me! You wish to be generous to those villains! Very well; I hope we mayn't repent it!"

"What danger shall we run," said Herbert, "if we take care to be always on our guard!"

"Hum!" observed the reporter, who had not given any decided opinion. "They are six and well-armed. If they each lay hid in a corner, and each fired at one of us, they would soon be masters of the colony!"

"Why have they not done so?" said Herbert. "No doubt because it was not their interest to do it. Besides, we are six also."

"Well, well!" replied Pencroft, whom no reasoning could have convinced. "Let us leave these good people to do what they like, and don't think anything more about them!"

"Come, Pencroft," said Neb, "don't make yourself out so bad as all that! Suppose one of these unfortunate men were here before you, within good range of your gun, you would not fire."

"I would fire on him as I would on a mad dog, Neb," replied Pencroft coldly.

"Pencroft," said the engineer, "you have always shown much deference to my advice; will you, in this matter, yield to me?"

"I will do as you please, Captain Harding," answered the sailor, who was not at all convinced.

"Very well, wait, and we will not attack them unless we are attacked first."

Thus their behaviour towards the pirates was agreed upon, although Pencroft augured nothing good from it. They were not to attack them, but were to be on their guard. After all, the island was large and fertile. If any sentiment of honesty yet remained in the bottom of their hearts, these wretches might perhaps be reclaimed. Was it not their interest in the situation in which they found themselves to begin a new life? At any rate, for humanity's sake alone, it would be right to wait. The colonists would no longer, as before, be able to go and come without fear. Hitherto they had only wild beasts to guard against, and now six convicts of the worst description, perhaps, were roaming over their island. It was serious, certainly, and to less brave men, it would have been security lost! No matter! At present, the colonists had reason on their side against Pencroft. Would they be right in the future? That remained to be seen.

VI

However, the chief business of the colonists was to make that complete exploration of the island which had been decided upon, and which would have two objects: to discover the mysterious being whose existence was now indisputable, and at the same time to find out what had become of the pirates, what retreat they had chosen, what sort of life they were leading, and what was to be feared from them. Cyrus Harding wished to set out without delay; but as the expedition would be of some days' duration, it appeared best to load the cart with different materials and tools in order to facilitate the organisation of the encampments. One of the onagers, however, having hurt its leg, could not be harnessed at present, and a few days' rest was necessary. The departure was, therefore, put off for a week, until the 20th of November. The month of November in this latitude corresponds to the month of May in the northern zones. It was, therefore, the fine season. The sun was entering the tropic of Capricorn, and gave the longest days in the year. The time was, therefore, very favourable for the projected expedition, which, if it did not accomplish its principal object, would at any rate be fruitful in discoveries, especially of natural productions, since Harding proposed to explore those dense forests of the Far West, which stretched to the extremity of the Serpentine Peninsula.

During the nine days which preceded their departure, it was agreed that the work on Prospect Heights should be finished off.

Moreover, it was necessary for Ayrton to return to the corral, where the domesticated animals required his care. It was decided that he should spend two days there, and return to Granite House after having liberally supplied the stables.

As he was about to start, Harding asked him if he would not like one of them to accompany him, observing that the island was less safe than formerly. Ayrton replied that this was unnecessary, as he was enough for the work, and that besides he apprehended no danger. If anything occurred at the corral, or in the neighbourhood, he could instantly warn the colonists by sending a telegram to Granite House.

Ayrton departed at dawn on the 9th, taking the cart drawn by one onager, and two hours after, the electric wire announced that he had found all in order at the corral.

During these two days Harding busied himself in executing a project which would completely guard Granite House against any surprise. It was necessary to completely conceal the opening of the old outlet, which was already walled up and partly hidden under grass and plants, at the southern angle of Lake Grant. Nothing was easier, since if the level of the lake was raised two or three feet, the opening would be quite beneath it. Now, to raise this level they had only to establish a dam at the two openings made by the lake, and by which were fed Creek Glycerine and Falls River.

The colonists worked with a will, and the two dams, which besides did not exceed eight feet in width by three in height, were rapidly erected by means of well-cemented blocks of stone.

This work finished, it would have been impossible to guess that at that part of the lake, there existed a subterranean passage through which the overflow of the lake formerly escaped.

Of course the little stream which fed the reservoir of Granite House and worked the lift had been carefully preserved, and the water could not fail. The lift once raised, this sure and comfortable retreat would be safe from any surprise.

This work had been so quickly done, that Pencroft, Gideon Spilett, and Herbert found time to make an expedition to Port Balloon. The sailor was very anxious to know if the little creek in which the *Bonadventure* was moored, had been visited by the convicts.

"These gentlemen," he observed, "landed on the south coast, and if they followed the shore, it is to be feared that they may have discovered the little harbour, and in that case, I wouldn't give half-a-dollar for our *Bonadventure*."

Pencroft's apprehensions were not without foundation, and a visit to Port Balloon appeared to be very desirable. The sailor and his companions set off on the 10th of November, after dinner, well-armed. Pencroft, ostentatiously slipping two bullets into each barrel of his rifle, shook his head in a way which betokened nothing good to any one who approached too near to him, whether "man or beast," as he said. Gideon

Spilett and Herbert also took their guns, and about three o'clock all three left Granite House.

Neb accompanied them to the turn of the Mercy, and after they had crossed, he raised the bridge. It was agreed that a gun-shot should announce the colonists' return, and that at the signal Neb should return and re-establish the communication between the two banks of the river.

The little band advanced directly along the road which led to the southern coast of the island. This was only a distance of three miles and a half, but Gideon Spilett and his companions took two hours to traverse it. They examined all the border of the road, the thick forest, as well as Tabor Marsh. They found no trace of the fugitives who, no doubt, not having yet discovered the number of the colonists, or the means of defence which they had at their disposal, had gained the less accessible parts of the island.

Arrived at Port Balloon, Pencroft saw with extreme satisfaction that the *Bonadventure* was tranquilly floating in the narrow creek. However, Port Balloon was so well hidden amongst high rocks that it could scarcely be discovered either from the land or the sea.

"Come," said Pencroft, "the blackguards have not been there yet. Long grass suits reptiles best, and evidently we shall find them in the Far West."

"And it's very lucky, for if they had found the *Bonadventure*," added Herbert, "they would have gone off in her, and we should have been prevented from returning to Tabor Island."

"Indeed," remarked the reporter, "it will be important to take a document there which will make known the situation of Lincoln Island, and Ayrton's new residence, in case the Scotch yacht returns to fetch him."

"Well, the *Bonadventure* is always there, Mr. Spilett," answered the sailor. "She and her crew are ready to start at a moment's notice!"

"I think, Pencroft, that that is a thing to be done after our exploration of the island is finished. It is possible after all that the stranger, if we manage to find him, may know as much about Tabor Island as about Lincoln Island. Do not forget that he is certainly the author of the document, and he may, perhaps, know how far we may count on the return of the yacht!"

"But!" exclaimed Pencroft, "who in the world can he be? The fellow knows us and we know nothing about him! If he is a simple castaway, why should he conceal himself? We are honest men, I suppose, and the society of honest men isn't unpleasant to any one. Did he come here voluntarily? Can he leave the island if he likes? Is he here still? Will he remain any longer?"

Chatting thus, Pencroft, Gideon Spilett, and Herbert got on board and looked about the deck of the *Bonadventure*. All at once, the sailor having examined the bitts to which the cable of the anchor was secured—

"Hallo," he cried, "this is queer!"

"What is the matter, Pencroft?" asked the reporter.

"The matter is, that it was not I who made this knot!"

And Pencroft showed a rope which fastened the cable to the bitt itself.

"What, it was not you?" asked Gideon Spilett.

"No! I can swear to it. This is a reef knot, and I always make a running bowline."

"You must be mistaken, Pencroft."

"I am not mistaken!" declared the sailor. "My hand does it so naturally, and one's hand is never mistaken!"

"Then can the convicts have been on board?" asked Herbert.

"I know nothing about that," answered Pencroft, "but what is certain, is that some one has weighed the *Bonadventure's* anchor and dropped it again! And look here, here is another proof! The cable of the anchor has been run out, and its service is no longer at the hawse-hole. I repeat that some one has been using our vessel!"

"But if the convicts had used her, they would have pillaged her, or rather gone off with her."

"Gone off! where to—to Tabor Island?" replied Pencroft. "Do you think they would risk themselves in a boat of such small tonnage?"

"We must, besides, be sure that they know of the islet," rejoined the reporter.

"However that may be," said the sailor, "as sure as my name is Bonadventure Pencroft, of the Vineyard, our *Bonadventure* has sailed without us!"

The sailor was so positive that neither Gideon Spilett nor Herbert could dispute his statement. It was evident that the vessel had been moved, more or less, since Pencroft had brought her to Port Balloon. As to the sailor, he had not the slightest doubt that the anchor had been raised and then dropped again. Now, what was the use of these two manoeuvres, unless the vessel had been employed in some expedition?

"But how was it we did not see the *Bonadventure* pass in sight of the island?" observed the reporter, who was anxious to bring forward every possible objection.

"Why, Mr. Spilett," replied the sailor, "they would only have to start in the night with a good breeze, and they would be out of sight of the island in two hours."

"Well," resumed Gideon Spilett, "I ask again, what object could the convicts have had in using the *Bonadventure*, and why, after they had made use of her, should they have brought her back to port?"

"Why, Mr. Spilett," replied the sailor, "we must put that among the unaccountable things, and not think anything more about it. The chief thing is that the *Bonadventure* was there, and she is there now. Only, unfortunately, if the convicts take her a second time, we shall very likely not find her again in her place!"

"Then, Pencroft," said Herbert, "would it not be wisest to bring the *Bonadventure* off to Granite House?"

"Yes and no," answered Pencroft, "or rather no. The mouth of the Mercy is a bad place for a vessel, and the sea is heavy there."

"But by hauling her up on the sand, to the foot of the Chimneys?"

"Perhaps yes," replied Pencroft. "At any rate, since we must leave Granite House for a long expedition, I think the *Bonadventure* will be safer here during our absence, and we shall do best to leave her here until the island is rid of these blackguards."

"That is exactly my opinion," said the reporter. "At any rate in the event of bad weather, she will not be exposed here as she would be at the mouth of the Mercy."

"But suppose the convicts pay her another visit," said Herbert.

"Well, my boy," replied Pencroft, "not finding her here, they would not be long in finding her on the sands of Granite House, and, during our absence, nothing could hinder them from seizing her! I agree, therefore, with Mr. Spilett, that she must be left in Port Balloon. But, if on our return we have not rid the island of those rascals, it will be prudent to bring our boat to Granite House, until the time when we need not fear any unpleasant visits."

"That's settled. Let us be off," said the reporter.

Pencroft, Herbert, and Gideon Spilett, on their return to Granite House, told the engineer all that had passed, and the latter approved of their arrangements both for the present and the future. He also promised the sailor that he would study that part of the channel situated between the islet and the coast; so as to ascertain if it would not be possible to make an artificial harbour there by means of dams. In this way, the *Bonadventure* would be always within reach, under the eyes of the colonists, and if necessary, under lock and key.

That evening a telegram was sent to Ayrton, requesting him to bring from the corral a couple of goats, which Neb wished to acclimatise to the plateau. Singularly enough, Ayrton did not acknowledge the receipt of the despatch, as he was accustomed to do. This could not but astonish the engineer. But it might be that Ayrton was not at that moment in the corral, or even that he was on his way back to Granite House. In fact, two days had already passed since his departure, and it had been decided that on the evening of the 10th or at the latest the morning of the 11th, he should return. The colonists waited, therefore, for Ayrton to appear on Prospect Heights. Neb and Herbert even watched at the bridge so as to be ready to lower it the moment their companion presented himself.

But up to ten in the evening, there were no signs of Ayrton. It was, therefore, judged best to send a fresh despatch, requiring an immediate reply.

The bell of the telegraph at Granite House remained mute.

The colonists' uneasiness was great. What had happened? Was Ayrton no longer at the corral, or if he was still there, had he no longer control over his movements? Could they go to the corral in this dark night?

They consulted. Some wished to go, the others to remain.

"But," said Herbert, "perhaps some accident had happened to the telegraphic apparatus, so that it works no longer?"

"That may be," said the reporter.

"Wait till to-morrow," replied Cyrus Harding. "It is possible, indeed, that Ayrton has not received our despatch, or even that we have not received his."

They waited, of course not without some anxiety.

At dawn of day, the 11th of November, Harding again sent the electric current along the wire and received no reply.

He tried again: the same result.

"Off to the corral," said he.

"And well-armed!" added Pencroft.

It was immediately decided that Granite House should not be left alone and that Neb should remain there. After having accompanied his friends to Creek Glycerine, he raised the bridge; and waiting behind a tree he watched for the return of either his companions or Ayrton.

In the event of the pirates presenting themselves and attempting to force the passage, he was to endeavour to stop them by firing on them, and as a last resource he was to take refuge in Granite House, where, the lift once raised, he would be in safety.

Cyrus Harding, Gideon Spilett, Herbert, and Pencroft were to repair to the corral, and if they did not find Ayrton, search the neighbouring woods.

At six o'clock in the morning, the engineer and his three companions had passed Creek Glycerine, and Neb posted himself behind a small mound crowned by several dragoniners on the left bank of the stream.

The colonists, after leaving the plateau of Prospect Heights, immediately took the road to the corral. They shouldered their guns, ready to fire on the smallest hostile demonstration. The two rifles and the two guns had been loaded with ball.

The wood was thick on each side of the road and might easily have concealed the convicts, who owing to their weapons would have been really formidable.

The colonists walked rapidly and in silence. Top preceded them, sometimes running on the road, sometimes taking a ramble into the wood, but always quiet and not appearing to fear anything unusual. And they could be sure that the faithful dog would not allow them to be surprised, but would bark at the least appearance of danger.

Cyrus Harding and his companions followed beside the road the wire which connected the corral with Granite House. After walking for nearly two miles, they had not as yet discovered any explanation of the difficulty. The posts were in good order, the wire regularly expended. However, at that moment the engineer observed that the wire appeared to be slack, and on arriving at post Number 74, Herbert, who was in advance stopped, exclaiming—

"The wire is broken!"

His companions hurried forward and arrived at the spot where the lad was standing. The post was rooted up and lying across the path. The unexpected explanation of the difficulty was here, and it was evident that the despatches from Granite House had not been received at the corral, nor those from the corral at Granite House.

"It wasn't the wind that blew down this post," observed Pencroft.

"No," replied Gideon Spilett. "The earth has been dug up round its foot, and it has been torn up by the hand of man."

"Besides, the wire is broken," added Herbert, showing that the wire had been snapped.

"Is the fracture recent?" asked Harding.

"Yes," answered Herbert, "it has certainly been done quite lately."

"To the corral! to the corral!" exclaimed the sailor.

The colonists were now half way between Granite House and the corral, having still two miles and a half to go. They pressed forward with redoubled speed.

Indeed, it was to be feared that some serious accident had occurred in the corral. No doubt, Ayrton might have sent a telegram which had not arrived, but this was not the reason why his companions were so uneasy, for, a more unaccountable circumstance, Ayrton, who had promised to return the evening before, had not reappeared. In short, it was not without a motive that all communication had been stopped between the corral and Granite House, and who but the convicts could have any interest in interrupting this communication?

The settlers hastened on, their hearts oppressed with anxiety. They were sincerely attached to their new companion. Were they to find him struck down by the hands of those of whom he was formerly the leader?

Soon they arrived at the place where the road led along the side of a little stream which flowed from the Red Creek and watered the meadows of the corral. They then moderated their pace so that they should not be out of breath at the moment when a struggle might be necessary. Their guns were in their hands ready cocked. The forest was watched on every side. Top uttered sullen groans which were rather ominous.

At last the palisade appeared through the trees. No trace of any damage could be seen. The gate was shut as usual. Deep silence reigned in the corral. Neither the accustomed bleating of the sheep nor Ayrton's voice could be heard.

"Let us enter," said Cyrus Harding.

And the engineer advanced, whilst his companions, keeping watch about twenty paces behind him, were ready to fire at a moment's notice.

Harding raised the inner latch of the gate and was about to push it back, when Top barked loudly. A report sounded and was responded to by a cry of pain.

Herbert, struck by a bullet, lay stretched on the ground.

VII

At Herbert's cry Pencroft, letting his gun fall, rushed towards him.
"They have killed him!" he cried. "My boy! They have killed him!"

Cyrus Harding and Gideon Spilett ran to Herbert.

The reporter listened to ascertain if the poor lad's heart was still beating.

"He lives," said he; "but he must be carried—"

"To Granite House? that is impossible!" replied the engineer.

"Into the corral, then!" said Pencroft.

"In a moment," said Harding.

And he ran round the left corner of the palisade. There he found a convict who, aiming at him, sent a ball through his hat. In a few seconds, before he had even time to fire his second barrel, he fell, struck to the heart by Harding's dagger, more sure even than his gun.

During this time, Gideon Spilett and the sailor hoisted themselves over the palisade, leapt into the enclosure, threw down the props which supported the inner door, ran into the empty house, and soon poor Herbert was lying on Ayrton's bed. In a few moments, Harding was by his side.

On seeing Herbert senseless, the sailor's grief was terrible. He sobbed, he cried, he tried to beat his head against the wall. Neither the engineer nor the reporter could calm him. They themselves were choked with emotion. They could not speak.

However, they knew that it depended on them to rescue from death the poor boy who was suffering beneath their eyes. Gideon Spilett had not passed through the many incidents by which his life had been chequered without acquiring some slight knowledge of medicine. He knew a little of everything, and several times he had been obliged to attend to wounds produced either by a sword-bayonet or shot. Assisted by Cyrus Harding, he proceeded to render the aid Herbert required.

The reporter was immediately struck by the complete stupor in which Herbert lay, a stupor owing either to the haemorrhage, or to the shock, the ball having struck a bone with sufficient force to produce a violent concussion.

Herbert was deadly pale, and his pulse so feeble that Spilett only felt it beat at long intervals, as if it was on the point of stopping. These symptoms were very serious. Herbert's chest was laid bare, and the blood having been staunched with handkerchiefs, it was bathed with cold water. The contusion, or rather the contused wound appeared,—an oval below the chest between the third and fourth ribs. It was there that Herbert had been hit by the bullet.

Cyrus Harding and Gideon Spilett then turned the poor boy over; as they did so, he uttered a moan so feeble that they almost thought it was his last sigh.

Herbert's back was covered with blood from another contused wound, by which the ball had immediately escaped.

"God be praised!" said the reporter, "the ball is not in the body, and we shall not have to extract it."

"But the heart?" asked Harding.

"The heart has not been touched; if it had been, Herbert would be dead!"

"Dead!" exclaimed Pencroft, with a groan. The sailor had only heard the last words uttered by the reporter.

"No, Pencroft," replied Cyrus Harding, "no! He is not dead. His pulse still beats. He has even uttered a moan. But for your boy's sake, calm yourself. We have need of all our self-possession. Do not make us lose it, my friend."

Pencroft was silent, but a reaction set in, and great tears rolled down his cheeks.

In the meanwhile, Gideon Spilett endeavoured to collect his ideas, and proceed methodically. After his examination he had no doubt that the ball, entering in front, between the seventh and eighth ribs, had issued behind between the third and fourth. But what mischief had the ball committed in its passage? What important organs had been reached? A professional surgeon would have had difficulty in determining this at once, and still more so the reporter.

However, he knew one thing, this was that he would have to prevent the inflammatory strangulation of the injured parts, then to contend with the local inflammation and fever which would result from the wound, perhaps mortal! Now, what stiptics, what antiphlogistics ought to be employed? By what means could inflammation be prevented?

At any rate, the most important thing was that the two wounds should be dressed without delay. It did not appear necessary to Gideon Spilett that a fresh flow of blood should be caused by bathing them in tepid water, and compressing their lips. The haemorrhage had been very abundant, and Herbert was already too much enfeebled by the loss of blood.

The reporter, therefore, thought it best to simply bathe the two wounds with cold water.

Herbert was placed on his left side, and was maintained in that position.

"He must not be moved," said Gideon Spilett. "He is in the most favourable position for the wounds in his back and chest to suppurate easily, and absolute rest is necessary."

"What! can't we carry him to Granite House?" asked Pencroft.

"No, Pencroft," replied the reporter.

"I'll pay the villains off!" cried the sailor, shaking his fist in a menacing manner.

"Pencroft!" said Cyrus Harding.

Gideon Spilett had resumed his examination of the wounded boy. Herbert was still so frightfully pale that the reporter felt anxious.

"Cyrus," said he, "I am not a surgeon. I am in terrible perplexity. You must aid me with your advice, your experience!"

"Take courage, my friend," answered the engineer, pressing the reporter's hand. "Judge coolly. Think only of this: Herbert must be saved!"

These words restored to Gideon Spilett that self-possession which he had lost in a moment of discouragement on feeling his great responsibility. He seated himself close to the bed. Cyrus Harding stood near. Pencroft had torn up his shirt, and was mechanically making lint.

Spilett then explained to Cyrus Harding that he thought he ought first of all to stop the haemorrhage, but not close the two wounds, or cause their immediate cicatrisation, for there had been internal perforation, and the suppuration must not be allowed to accumulate in the chest.

Harding approved entirely, and it was decided that the two wounds should be dressed without attempting to close them by immediate coaptation.

And now, did the colonists possess an efficacious agent to act against the inflammation which might occur?

Yes. They had one, for nature had generously lavished it. They had cold water, that is to say, the most powerful sedative that can be employed against inflammation of wounds, the most efficacious therapeutic agent in grave cases, and the one which is now adopted by all physicians. Cold water has, moreover, the advantage of leaving the wound in absolute rest, and preserving it from all premature dressing, a considerable advantage, since it has been found by experience that contact with the air is dangerous during the first days.

Gideon Spilett and Cyrus Harding reasoned thus with their simple good sense, and they acted as the best surgeon would have done. Compresses of linen were applied to poor Herbert's two wounds, and were kept constantly wet with cold water.

The sailor had at first lighted a fire in the hut, which was not wanting in things necessary for life. Maple sugar, medicinal plants, the same which the lad had gathered on the banks of Lake Grant, enabled them to make some refreshing drinks, which they gave him without his taking any notice of it. His fever was extremely high, and all that day and night passed without his becoming conscious.

Herbert's life hung on a thread, and this thread might break at any moment. The next day, the 12th of November, the hopes of Harding and his companions slightly revived. Herbert had come out of his long stupor. He opened his eyes, he recognised Cyrus Harding, the reporter, and Pencroft. He uttered two or three words. He did not know what had happened. They told him, and Spilett begged him to remain perfectly still, telling him that his life was not in danger, and that his wounds would heal in a few days. However, Herbert scarcely suffered at all, and the cold water with which they were constantly bathed, prevented any inflammation of the wounds. The suppuration was established in a regular way, the fever did not increase, and it might now be hoped that this terrible wound would not involve any catastrophe. Pencroft felt the swelling of his heart gradually subside. He was like a sister of mercy, like a mother by the bed of her child.

Herbert dozed again, but his sleep appeared more natural.

"Tell me again that you hope, Mr. Spilett," said Pencroft. "Tell me again that you will save Herbert!"

"Yes, we will save him!" replied the reporter. "The wound is serious, and, perhaps, even the ball has traversed the lungs, but the perforation of this organ is not fatal."

"God bless you!" answered Pencroft.

As may be believed, during the four-and-twenty hours they had been in the corral, the colonists had no other thought than that of nursing Herbert. They did not think either of the danger which threatened them should the convicts return, or of the precautions to be taken for the future.

But on this day, whilst Pencroft watched by the sick-bed, Cyrus Harding and the reporter consulted as to what it would be best to do.

First of all they examined the corral. There was not a trace of Ayrton. Had the unhappy man been dragged away by his former accomplices? Had he resisted, and been overcome in the struggle? This last supposition was only too probable. Gideon Spilett, at the moment he scaled the palisade, had clearly seen some one of the convicts running along the southern spur of Mount Franklin, towards whom Top had sprung. It was one of those whose object had been so completely defeated by the rocks at the mouth of the Mercy. Besides, the one killed by Harding, and whose body was found outside the enclosure, of course belonged to Bob Harvey's crew.

As to the corral, it had not suffered any damage. The gates were closed, and the animals had not been able to disperse in the forest. Nor could they see traces of any struggle, any devastation, either in the hut, or in the palisade. The ammunition only, with which Ayrton had been supplied, had disappeared with him.

"The unhappy man has been surprised," said Harding, "and as he was a man to defend himself, he must have been overpowered."

"Yes, that is to be feared!" said the reporter. "Then, doubtless, the convicts installed themselves in the corral where they found plenty of everything, and only fled when they saw us coming. It is very evident, too, that at this moment Ayrton, whether living or dead, is not here!"

"We shall have to beat the forest," said the engineer, "and rid the island of these wretches. Pencroft's presentiments were not mistaken, when he wished to hunt them as wild beasts. That would have spared us all these misfortunes!"

"Yes," answered the reporter, "but now we have the right to be merciless!"

"At any rate," said the engineer, "we are obliged to wait some time, and to remain at the corral until we can carry Herbert without danger to Granite House."

"But Neb?" asked the reporter.

"Neb is in safety."

"But if, uneasy at our absence, he would venture to come?"

"He must not come!" returned Cyrus Harding quickly. "He would be murdered on the road!"

"It is very probable, however, that he will attempt to rejoin us!"

"Ah, if the telegraph still acted, he might be warned! But that is impossible now! As to leaving Pencroft and Herbert here alone, we could not do it! Well, I will go alone to Granite House."

"No, no! Cyrus," answered the reporter, "you must not expose yourself! Your courage would be of no avail. The villains are evidently watching the corral, they are hidden in the thick woods which surround it, and if you go we shall soon have to regret two misfortunes instead of one!"

"But Neb?" repeated the engineer. "It is now four-and-twenty hours since he has had any news of us! He will be sure to come!"

"And as he will be less on his guard than we should be ourselves," added Spilett, "he will be killed!"

"Is there really no way of warning him?"

Whilst the engineer thought, his eyes fell on Top, who, going backwards and forwards, seemed to say—

"Am not I here?"

"Top!" exclaimed Cyrus Harding.

The animal sprang at his master's call.

"Yes, Top will go," said the reporter, who had understood the engineer. "Top can go where we cannot! He will carry to Granite House the news of the corral, and he will bring back to us that from Granite House!"

"Quick!" said Harding. "Quick!"

Spilett rapidly tore a leaf from his notebook, and wrote these words:—

"Herbert wounded. We are at the corral. Be on your guard. Do not leave Granite House. Have the convicts appeared in the neighbourhood? Reply by Top."

This laconic note contained all that Neb ought to know, and at the same time asked all the colonists wished to know. It was folded and fastened to Top's collar in a conspicuous position.

"Top, my dog," said the engineer, caressing the animal, "Neb, Top! Neb! Go, go!"

Top bounded at these words. He understood, he knew what was expected of him. The road to the corral was familiar to him. In less than an hour he could clear it, and it might be hoped that where neither Cyrus Harding nor the reporter could have ventured without danger, Top, running amongst the grass or in the wood, would pass unperceived.

The engineer went to the gate of the corral and opened it.

"Neb, Top! Neb!" repeated the engineer, again pointing in the direction of Granite House.

Top sprang forwards, and almost immediately disappeared.

"He will get there!" said the reporter.

"Yes, and he will come back, the faithful animal!"

"What o'clock is it?" asked Gideon Spilett.

"Ten."

"In an hour he may be here. We will watch for his return."

The gate of the corral was closed. The engineer and the reporter re-entered the house. Herbert was still in a sleep. Pencroft kept the compresser always wet. Spilett, seeing there was nothing he could do at that moment, busied himself in preparing some nourishment, whilst attentively watching that part of the enclosure against the hill, at which an attack might be expected.

The settlers awaited Top's return with much anxiety. A little before eleven o'clock, Cyrus Harding and the reporter, rifle in hand, were behind the gate, ready to open it at the first bark of their dog.

They did not doubt that if Top had arrived safely at Granite House, Neb would have sent him back immediately.

They had both been there for about ten minutes, when a report was heard, followed by repeated barks.

The engineer opened the gate, and seeing smoke a hundred feet off in the wood, he fired in that direction.

Almost immediately Top bounded into the corral, and the gate was quickly shut.

"Top, Top!" exclaimed the engineer, taking the dog's great honest head between his hands.

A note was fastened to his neck, and Cyrus Harding read these words, traced in Neb's large writing:—

"No pirates in the neighbourhood of Granite House. I will not stir. Poor Mr. Herbert!"

VIII

So the convicts were still there, watching the corral, and determined to kill the settlers one after the other. There was nothing to be done but to treat them as wild beasts. But great precautions must be taken, for just now the wretches had the advantage on their side, seeing, and not being seen, being able to surprise by the suddenness of their attack, yet not to be surprised themselves. Harding made arrangements, therefore, for living in the corral, of which the provisions would last for a tolerable length of time. Ayrton's house had been provided with all that was necessary for existence, and the convicts, scared by the arrival of the settlers, had not had time to pillage it. It was probable, as Gideon Spilett observed, that things had occurred as follows:—The six convicts, disembarking on the island, had followed the southern shore, and after having traversed the double shore of the Serpentine Peninsula, not being inclined to venture into the Far West woods, they had reached the mouth of Falls River. From this point, by following the right bank of the watercourse, they would arrive at the spurs of Mount Franklin, among which they would naturally seek a retreat, and they could not have been long in discovering the corral, then uninhabited. There they had regularly installed themselves, awaiting the moment to put their abominable schemes into execution. Ayrton's arrival had surprised them, but they had managed to overpower the unfortunate man, and—the rest may be easily imagined!

Now, the convicts,—reduced to five, it is true, but well-armed,— were roaming the woods, and to venture there was to expose themselves to their attacks, which could be neither guarded against nor prevented.

"Wait! There is nothing else to be done!" repeated Cyrus Harding. "When Herbert is cured, we can organise a general battue of the island, and have satisfaction of these convicts. That will be the object of our grand expedition at the same time—"

"As the search for our mysterious protector," added Gideon Spilett, finishing the engineer's sentence. "Ah, it must be acknowledged, my dear Cyrus, that this time his protection was wanting at the very moment when it was most necessary to us!"

"Who knows?" replied the engineer.

"What do you mean?" asked the reporter.

"That we are not at the end of our trouble yet, my dear Spilett, and that his powerful invention may, perhaps, have another opportunity of exercising itself. But that is not the question now. Herbert's life before everything."

This was the colonists' saddest thought. Several days passed, and the poor boy's state was happily no worse. Cold water, always kept at a suitable temperature, had completely prevented the inflammation of the wounds. It even seemed to the reporter that this water, being slightly sulphurous,—which was explained by the neighbourhood of the volcano,—had a more direct action on the healing. The suppuration was much less abundant, and—thanks to the incessant care by which he was surrounded!—Herbert returned to life, and his fever abated. He was besides subjected to a severe diet, and consequently his weakness was and would be extreme; but there was no want of refreshing drinks, and absolute rest was of the greatest benefit to him. Cyrus Harding, Gideon Spilett, and Pencroft had become very skilful in dressing the lad's wounds. All the linen in the house had been sacrificed. Herbert's wounds, covered with compresses and lint, were pressed neither too much nor too little, so as to cause their cicatrisation without determining on inflammatory reaction. The reporter used extreme care in the dressing, knowing well the importance of it, and repeating to his companions that which most surgeons willingly admit, that it is perhaps rarer to see a dressing well done than an operation well performed.

In ten days, on the 22nd of November, Herbert was considerably better. He had begun to take some nourishment. The colour was returning to his cheeks, and his bright eyes smiled at his nurses. He talked a little, notwithstanding Pencraft's efforts, who talked incessantly to prevent him from beginning to speak, and told him the most improbable stories. Herbert had questioned him on the subject of Ayrton, whom he was astonished not to see near him, thinking that he was at the corral. But the sailor, not wishing to distress Herbert, contented himself by replying that Ayrton had rejoined Neb, so as to defend Granite House.

"Humph!" said Pencroft, "these pirates! they are gentlemen who have no right to any consideration! And the captain wanted to win them by kindness! I'll send them some kindness, but in the shape of a good bullet!"

"And have they not been seen again?" asked Herbert.

"No, my boy," answered the sailor, "but we shall find them, and when you are cured we shall see if the cowards, who strike us from behind, will dare to meet us face to face!"

"I am still very weak, my poor Pencroft!"

"Well! your strength will return gradually! What's a ball through the chest? Nothing but a joke! I've seen many, and I don't think much of them!"

At last things appeared to be going on well, and if no complication occurred, Herbert's recovery might be regarded as certain. But what would have been the condition of the colonists if his state had been aggravated,—if, for example, the ball had remained in his body, if his arm or his leg had had to be amputated?

"No," said Spilett more than once, "I have never thought of such a contingency without shuddering!"

"And yet, if it had been necessary to operate," said Harding one day to him, "you would not have hesitated?"

"No, Cyrus!" said Gideon Spilett, "but thank God that we have been spared this complication!"

As in so many other conjectures, the colonists had appealed to the logic of that simple good sense of which they had made use so often, and once more, thanks to their general knowledge, it had succeeded! But might not a time come when all their science would be at fault? They were alone on the island. Now, men in all states of society are necessary to each other. Cyrus Harding knew this well, and sometimes he asked himself if some circumstance might not occur which they would be powerless to surmount. It appeared to him besides, that he and his companions, till then so fortunate, had entered into an unlucky period. During the three years and a half which had elapsed since their escape from Richmond, it might be said that they had had everything their own way. The island had abundantly supplied them with minerals, vegetables, animals, and as Nature had constantly loaded them, their science had known how to take advantage of what she offered them.

The well-being of the colony was therefore complete. Moreover, in certain occurrences an inexplicable influence had come to their aid! . . . But all that could only be for a time.

In short, Cyrus Harding believed that fortune had turned against them.

In fact, the convicts' ship had appeared in the waters of the island, and if the pirates had been, so to speak, miraculously destroyed, six of them, at least, had escaped the catastrophe. They had disembarked on the island, and it was almost impossible to get at the five who survived. Ayrton had no doubt been murdered by these wretches, who possessed fire-arms, and at the first use that they had made of them, Herbert had fallen, wounded almost mortally. Were these the first blows aimed by adverse fortune at the colonists? This was often asked by Harding. This was often repeated by the reporter; and it appeared to him also that the intervention, so strange, yet so efficacious, which till then had served them so well, had now failed them. Had this mysterious being, whatever he was, whose existence could not be denied, abandoned the island? Had he in his turn succumbed?

No reply was possible to these questions. But it must not be imagined that because Harding and his companion spoke of these things, they were men to despair. Far from that. They looked their situation in the face, they analysed the chances, they prepared themselves for any event, they stood firm and straight before the future, and if adversity was at last to strike them, it would find in them men prepared to struggle against it.

IX

No News of Neb—A Proposal from Pencroft and the
Reporter, which is not accepted—Several Sorties by
Gideon Spilett—A Rag of Cloth—A Message—Hasty
Departure—Arrival on the Plateau of Prospect Heights.

The convalescence of the young invalid was regularly progressing. One thing only was now to be desired, that his state would allow him to be brought to Granite House. However well built and supplied the corral house was, it could not be so comfortable as the healthy granite dwelling. Besides, it did not offer the same security, and its tenants, notwithstanding their watchfulness, were here always in fear of some shot from the convicts. There, on the contrary, in the middle of that impregnable and inaccessible cliff, they would have nothing to fear, and any attack on their persons would certainly fail. They therefore waited impatiently for the moment when Herbert might be moved without danger from his wound, and they were determined to make this move, although the communication through Jacamar Wood was very difficult.

They had no news from Neb, but were not uneasy on that account. The courageous negro, well intrenched in the depths of Granite House, would not allow himself to be surprised. Top had not been sent again to him, as it appeared useless to expose the faithful dog to some shot which might deprive the settlers of their most useful auxiliary.

They waited, therefore, although they were anxious to be reunited at Granite House. It pained the engineer to see his forces divided, for it gave great advantage to the pirates. Since Ayrton's disappearance they were only four against five, for Herbert could not yet be counted, and this was not the least care of the brave boy, who well understood the trouble of which he was the cause.

The question of knowing how, in their condition, they were to act against the pirates, was thoroughly discussed on the 29th of November by Cyrus Harding, Gideon Spilett, and Pencroft, at a moment when Herbert was asleep and could not hear them.

"My friends," said the reporter, after they had talked of Neb and of the impossibility of communicating with him, "I think, like you, that to venture on the road to the corral would be to risk receiving a gun-shot without being able to return it. But do you not think that the best thing to be done now is to openly give chase to these wretches?"

"That is just what I was thinking," answered Pencroft. "I believe we're not fellows to be afraid of a bullet, and as for me, if Captain Harding approves, I'm ready to dash into the forest! Why, hang it, one man is equal to another!"

"But is he equal to five?" asked the engineer.

"I will join Pencroft," said the reporter, "and both of us, well-armed and accompanied by Top—"

"My dear Spilett, and you, Pencroft," answered Harding, "let us reason coolly. If the convicts were hid in one spot of the island, if we knew that spot, and had only to dislodge them, I would undertake a direct attack; but is there not occasion to fear, on the contrary, that they are sure to fire the first shot."

"Well, captain," cried Pencroft, "a bullet does not always reach its mark."

"That which struck Herbert did not miss, Pencroft," replied the engineer. "Besides, observe that if both of you left the corral I should remain here alone to defend it. Do you imagine that the convicts will not see you leave it, that they will not allow you to enter the forest, and that they will not attack it during your absence, knowing that there is no one here but a wounded boy and a man?"

"You are right, captain," replied Pencroft, his chest swelling with sullen anger. "You are right; they will do all they can to retake the corral, which they know to be well stored; and alone you could not hold it against them."

"Oh, if we were only at Granite House!"

"If we were at Granite House," answered the engineer, "the case would be very different. There I should not be afraid to leave Herbert with one, whilst the other three went to search the forests of the island. But we are at the corral, and it is best to stay here until we can leave it together."

Cyrus Harding's reasoning was unanswerable, and his companions understood it well.

"If only Ayrton was still one of us!" said Gideon Spilett. "Poor fellow! his return to social life will have been but of short duration."

"If he is dead," added Pencroft, in a peculiar tone.

"Do you hope, then, Pencroft, that the villains have spared him?" asked Gideon Spilett.

"Yes, if they had any interest in doing so."

"What! you suppose that Ayrton, finding his old companions, forgetting all that he owes us—"

"Who knows?" answered the sailor, who did not hazard this shameful supposition without hesitating.

"Pencroft," said Harding, taking the sailor's arm, "that is a wicked idea of yours, and you will distress me much if you persist in speaking thus. I will answer for Ayrton's fidelity."

"And I also," added the reporter quickly.

"Yes, yes, captain, I was wrong," replied Pencroft; "it was a wicked idea indeed that I had, and nothing justifies it. But what can I do? I'm not in my senses. This imprisonment in the corral wearies me horribly, and I have never felt so excited as I do now."

"Be patient, Pencroft," replied the engineer. "How long will it be, my dear Spilett, before you think Herbert may be carried to Granite House?"

"That is difficult to say, Cyrus," answered the reporter, "for any imprudence might involve terrible consequences. But his convalescence is progressing, and if he continues to gain strength, in eight days from now—well, we shall see."

Eight days! That would put off the return to Granite House until the first days of December. At this time two months of spring had already passed. The weather was fine, and the heat began to be great. The forests of the island were in full leaf, and the time was approaching when the usual crops ought to be gathered. The return to the plateau of Prospect Heights would, therefore, be followed by extensive agricultural labours, interrupted only by the projected expedition through the island.

It can, therefore, be well understood how injurious this seclusion in the corral must be to the colonists.

But if they were compelled to bow before necessity, they did not do so without impatience.

Once or twice the reporter ventured out into the road and made the tour of the palisade. Top accompanied him, and Gideon Spilett, his gun cocked, was ready for any emergency.

He met with no misadventure and found no suspicious traces. His dog would have warned him of any danger, and, as Top did not bark, it might be concluded that there was nothing to fear at that moment at least, and that the convicts were occupied in another part of the island.

However, on his second sortie, on the 27th of November, Gideon Spilett, who had ventured a quarter of a mile into the wood, towards the south of the mountains, remarked that Top scented something. The dog had no longer his unconcerned manner; he went backwards and forwards, ferreting amongst the grass and bushes as if his smell had revealed some suspicious object to him.

Gideon Spilett followed Top, encouraged him, excited him by his voice, whilst keeping a sharp look-out, his gun ready to fire, and sheltering himself behind the trees. It was not probable that Top scented the presence of man, for in that case, he would have announced it by half-uttered, sullen, angry barks. Now, as he did not growl, it was because danger was neither near nor approaching.

Nearly five minutes passed thus, Top rummaging, the reporter following him prudently, when, all at once, the dog rushed towards a thick bush, and drew out a rag.

It was a piece of cloth, stained and torn, which Spilett immediately brought back to the corral. There it was examined by the colonists, who found that it was a fragment of Ayrton's waistcoat, a piece of that felt, manufactured solely by the Granite House factory.

"You see, Pencroft," observed Harding, "there has been resistance on the part of the unfortunate Ayrton. The convicts have dragged him away in spite of himself! Do you still doubt his honesty?"

"No, captain," answered the sailor, "and I repented of my suspicion a long time ago! But it seems to me that something may be learned from the incident."

"What is that?" asked the reporter.

"It is that Ayrton was not killed at the corral! That they dragged him away living, since he has resisted. Therefore, perhaps, he is still living!"

"Perhaps, indeed," replied the engineer, who remained thoughtful.

This was a hope, to which Ayrton's companions could still hold. Indeed, they had before believed that, surprised in the corral, Ayrton had fallen by a bullet, as Herbert had fallen. But if the convicts had not killed him at first, if they had brought him living to another part of the island, might it not be admitted that he was still their prisoner? Perhaps, even, one of them had found in Ayrton his old Australian companion Ben Joyce, the chief of the escaped convicts. And who knows but that they had conceived the impossible hope of bringing back Ayrton to themselves? He would have been very useful to them, if they had been able to make him turn traitor!

This incident was, therefore, favourably interpreted at the corral, and it no longer appeared impossible that they should find Ayrton again. On his side, if he was only a prisoner, Ayrton would no doubt do all he could to escape from the hands of the villains, and this would be a powerful aid to the settlers!

"At any rate," observed Gideon Spilett, "if happily Ayrton did manage to escape, he would go directly to Granite House, for he could not know of the attempt of assassination of which Herbert has been a victim, and consequently would never think of our being imprisoned in the corral!"

"Oh! I wish that he was there, at Granite House!" cried Pencroft, "and that we were there, too! For, although the rascals can do nothing to our house, they may plunder the plateau, our plantations, our poultry-yard!"

Pencroft had become a thorough farmer, heartily attached to his crops. But it must be said that Herbert was more anxious than any to return to Granite House, for he knew how much the presence of the settlers was needed there. And it was he who was keeping them at the corral! Therefore, one idea occupied his mind—to leave the corral, and when! He believed he could bear removal to Granite House. He was sure his strength would return more quickly in his room, with the air and sight of the sea!

Several times he pressed Gideon Spilett, but the latter, fearing, with good reason, that Herbert's wounds, half healed, might reopen on the way, did not give the order to start.

However, something occurred which compelled Cyrus Harding and his two friends to yield to the lad's wish, and God alone knew that this determination might cause them grief and remorse.

It was the 29th of November, seven o'clock in the evening. The three settlers were talking in Herbert's room, when they heard Top utter quick barks.

Harding, Pencroft, and Spilett seized their guns and ran out of the house. Top, at the foot of the palisade, was jumping, barking, but it was with pleasure, not anger.

"Some one is coming."

"Yes."

"It is not an enemy!"

"Neb, perhaps?"

"Or Ayrton?"

These words had hardly been exchanged between the engineer and his two companions when a body leapt over the palisade and fell on the ground inside the corral.

It was Tup, Master Jup in person, to whom Top immediately gave a most cordial reception.

"Jup!" exclaimed Pencroft.

"Neb has sent him to us," said the reporter.

"Then," replied the engineer, "he must have some note on him."

Pencroft rushed up to the orang. Certainly if Neb had any important matter to communicate to his master he could not employ a more sure or more rapid messenger, who could pass where neither the colonists could, nor even Top himself.

Cyrus Harding was not mistaken. At Jup's neck hung a small bag, and in this bag was found a little note traced by Neb's hand.

The despair of Harding and his companions may be imagined when they read these words:—

"Friday, six o'clock in the morning.

"Plateau invaded by convicts.

"Neb."

They gazed at each other without uttering a word, then they re-entered the house. What were they to do? The convicts on Prospect Heights! that was disaster, devastation, ruin.

Herbert, on seeing the engineer, the reporter, and Pencroft re-enter, guessed that their situation was aggravated, and when he saw Jup, he no longer doubted that some misfortune menaced Granite House.

"Captain Harding," said he, "I must go; I can bear the journey. I must go."

Gideon Spilett approached Herbert; then, having looked at him—

"Let us go, then!" said he.

The question was quickly decided whether Herbert should be carried on a litter or in the cart which had brought Ayrton to the corral. The motion of the litter would have been more easy for the wounded lad, but it would have necessitated two bearers, that is to say, there would have been two guns less for defence if an attack was made on the road. Would they not, on the contrary, by employing the cart leave every arm free? Was it impossible to place the mattress on which Herbert was lying in it, and to advance with so much care than any jolt should be avoided? It could be done.

The cart was brought. Pencroft harnessed the onaga. Cyrus Harding and the reporter raised Herbert's mattress and placed it on the bottom of the cart. The weather was fine. The sun's bright rays glanced through the trees.

"Are the guns ready?" asked Cyrus Harding.

They were. The engineer and Pencroft, each armed with a double-barrelled gun, and Gideon Spilett carrying his rifle, had nothing to do but start.

"Are you comfortable, Herbert?" asked the engineer.

"Ah, captain," replied the lad, "don't be uneasy, I shall not die on the road!"

Whilst speaking thus, it could be seen that the poor boy had called up all his energy, and by the energy of a powerful will had collected his failing strength.

The engineer felt his heart sink painfully. He still hesitated to give the signal for departure; but that would have driven Herbert to despair—killed him perhaps.

"Forward!" said Harding.

The gate of the corral was opened. Jup and Top, who knew when to be silent, ran in advance. The cart came out, the gate was reclosed, and the onaga, led by Pencroft, advanced at a slow pace.

Certainly, it would have been safer to have taken a different road than that which led straight from the corral to Granite House, but the cart would have met with great difficulties in moving under the trees. It was necessary, therefore, to follow this way, although it was well-known to the convicts.

Cyrus Harding and Gideon Spilett walked one on each side of the cart, ready to answer to any attack. However, it was not probable that the convicts would have yet left the plateau of Prospect Heights.

Neb's note had evidently been written and sent as soon as the convicts had shown themselves there. Now, this note was dated six o'clock in the morning, and the active orang, accustomed to come frequently to the corral, had taken scarcely three quarters of an hour to cross the five miles which separated it from Granite House. They would, therefore, be safe at that time, and if there was any occasion for firing, it would probably not be until they were in the neighbourhood of Granite House. However, the colonists kept a strict watch. Top and Jup, the latter armed with his club, sometimes in front, sometimes beating the wood at the sides of the road, signalised no danger.

JULES VERNE (TRANSLATION FROM W.H.G. KINGSTON)

The cart advanced slowly under Pencroft's guidance. It had left the corral at half-past seven. An hour after four out of the five miles had been cleared, without any incident having occurred. The road was as deserted as all that part of the Jacamar Wood which lay between the Mercy and the lake. There was no occasion for any warning. The wood appeared as deserted as on the day when the colonists first landed on the island.

They approached the plateau. Another mile and they would see the bridge over Creek Glycerine. Cyrus Harding expected to find it in its place; supposing that the convicts; would have crossed it, and that, after having passed one of the streams which enclosed the plateau, they would have taken the precaution to lower it again, so as to keep open a retreat.

At length an opening in the trees allowed the sea-horizon to be seen. But the cart continued its progress, for not one of its defenders thought of abandoning it.

At that moment Pencroft stopped the onaga, and in a hoarse voice—

"Oh! the villains!" he exclaimed.

And he pointed to a thick smoke rising from the mill, the sheds, and the buildings at the poultry-yard.

A man was moving about in the midst of the smoke. It was Neb.

His companions uttered a shout. He heard, and ran to meet them.

The convicts had left the plateau nearly half-an-hour before, having devastated it!

"And Mr. Herbert?" asked Neb.

Gideon Spilett returned to the cart.

Herbert had lost consciousness!

X

Herbert carried to Granite House—Neb relates all that
has happened—Harding's Visit to the Plateau—Ruin and
Devastation—The Colonists baffled by Herbert's Illness—
Willow Bark—A Deadly Fever—Top barks again!

Of the convicts, the dangers which menaced Granite House, the
ruins with which the plateau was covered, the colonists thought
no longer. Herbert's critical state outweighed all other considerations.
Would the removal prove fatal to him by causing some internal injury?
The reporter could not affirm it, but he and his companions almost
despaired of the result. The cart was brought to the bend of the river.
There some branches, disposed as a litter, received the mattress on which
lay the unconscious Herbert. Ten minutes after, Cyrus Harding, Spilett,
and Pencroft were at the foot of the cliff, leaving Neb to take the cart
onto the plateau of Prospect Heights. The lift was put in motion, and
Herbert was soon stretched on his bed in Granite House.

What cares were lavished on him to bring him back to life! He
smiled for a moment on finding himself in his room, but could scarcely
even murmur a few words, so great was his weakness. Gideon Spilett
examined his wounds. He feared to find them reopened, having been
imperfectly healed. There was nothing of the sort. From whence, then,
came this prostration? Why was Herbert so much worse? The lad
then fell into a kind of feverish sleep, and the reporter and Pencroft
remained near the bed. During this time, Harding told Neb all that had
happened at the corral, and Neb recounted to his master the events of
which the plateau had just been the theatre.

It was only during the preceding night that the convicts had appeared
on the edge of the forest, at the approaches to Creek Glycerine. Neb,
who was watching near the poultry-yard, had not hesitated to fire at one
of the pirates, who was about to cross the stream; but in the darkness he
could not tell whether the man had been hit or not. At any rate, it was
not enough to frighten away the band, and Neb had only just time to
get up to Granite House, where at least he was in safety.

But what was he to do there? How prevent the devastations with
which the convicts threatened the plateau? Had Neb any means by which
to warn his master? And, besides, in what situation were the inhabitants

of the corral themselves? Cyrus Harding and his companions had left on the 11th of November, and it was now the 29th. It was, therefore, nineteen days since Neb had had other news than that brought by Top—disastrous news: Ayrton disappeared, Herbert severely wounded, the engineer, reporter, and sailor, as it were, imprisoned in the corral!

What was he to do? asked poor Neb. Personally he had nothing to fear, for the convicts could not reach him in Granite House. But the buildings, the plantations, all their arrangements at the mercy of the pirates! Would it not be best to let Cyrus Harding judge of what he ought to do, and to warn him, at least, of the danger which threatened him?

Neb then thought of employing Jup, and confiding a note to him. He knew the orang's great intelligence, which had been often put to the proof. Jup understood the word corral, which had been frequently pronounced before him, and it may be remembered, too, that he had often driven the cart thither in company with Pencroft. Day had not yet dawned. The active orang would know how to pass unperceived through the woods, of which the convicts, besides, would think he was a native.

Neb did not hesitate. He wrote the note, he tied it to Jup's neck, he brought the ape to the door of Granite House, from which he let down a long cord to the ground; then, several times, he repeated these words—

"Jup, Jup! corral, corral!"

The creature understood, seized the cord, glided rapidly down to the beach, and disappeared in the darkness without the convicts' attention having been in the least excited.

"You did well, Neb," said Harding; "but perhaps in not warning us you would have done still better!"

And, in speaking thus, Cyrus Harding thought of Herbert, whose recovery the removal had so seriously checked.

Neb ended his account. The convicts had not appeared at all on the beach. Not knowing the number of the island's inhabitants, they might suppose that Granite House was defended by a large party. They must have remembered that during the attack by the brig numerous shot had been fired both from the lower and upper rocks, and no doubt they did not wish to expose themselves. But the plateau of Prospect Heights was open to them, and not covered by the fire of Granite House. They gave themselves up, therefore, to their instinct of destruction,—plundering, burning, devastating everything,—and only retiring half an hour before the arrival of the colonists, whom they believed still confined in the corral.

On their retreat, Neb hurried out. He climbed the plateau at the risk of being perceived and fired at, tried to extinguish the fire which was consuming the buildings of the poultry-yard, and had struggled, though in vain, against it until the cart appeared at the edge of the wood.

Such had been these serious events. The presence of the convicts constituted a permanent source of danger to the settlers in Lincoln Island, until then so happy, and who might now expect still greater misfortunes.

Spilett remained in Granite House with Herbert and Pencroft, while Cyrus Harding, accompanied by Neb, proceeded to judge for himself of the extent of the disaster.

It was fortunate that the convicts had not advanced to the foot of Granite House. The workshop at the Chimneys would in that case not have escaped destruction. But after all, this evil would have been more easily reparable than the ruins accumulated on the plateau of Prospect Heights. Harding and Neb proceeded towards the Mercy, and ascended its left bank without meeting with any trace of the convicts; nor on the other side of the river, in the depths of the wood, could they perceive any suspicious indications.

Besides, it might be supposed that in all probability either the convicts knew of the return of the settlers to Granite House, by having seen them pass on the road from the corral, or, after the devastation of the plateau, they had penetrated into Jacamar Wood, following the course of the Mercy, and were thus ignorant of their return.

In the former case, they must have returned towards the corral, now without defenders, and which contained valuable stores.

In the latter, they must have regained their encampment, and would wait an opportunity to recommence the attack.

It was, therefore, possible to prevent them, but any enterprise to clear the island was now rendered difficult by reason of Herbert's condition. Indeed, their whole force would have been barely sufficient to cope with the convicts, and just now no one could leave Granite House.

The engineer and Neb arrived on the plateau. Desolation reigned everywhere. The fields had been trampled over; the ears of wheat, which were nearly full grown, lay on the ground. The other plantations had not suffered less.

The kitchen-garden was destroyed. Happily, Granite House possessed a store of seed which would enable them to repair these misfortunes.

As to the wall and buildings of the poultry-yard and the onagas' stable, the fire had destroyed all. A few terrified creatures roamed over the plateau. The birds, which during the fire had taken refuge on the waters of the lake, had already returned to their accustomed spot, and were dabbling on the banks. Everything would have to be reconstructed.

Cyrus Harding's face, which was paler than usual, expressed an internal anger which he commanded with difficulty, but he did not utter a word. Once more he looked at his devastated fields, and at the smoke which still rose from the ruins, then he returned to Granite House.

The following days were the saddest of any that the colonists had passed on the island! Herbert's weakness visibly increased. It appeared that a more serious malady, the consequence of the profound physiological disturbance he had gone through, threatened to declare itself, and Gideon Spilett feared such an aggravation of his condition that he would be powerless to fight against it!

In fact, Herbert remained in an almost continuous state of drowsiness, and symptoms of delirium began to manifest themselves. Refreshing drinks were the only remedies at the colonists' disposal. The fever was not as yet very high, but it soon appeared that it would probably recur at regular intervals. Gideon Spilett first recognised this on the 6th of December.

The poor boy, whose fingers, nose, and ears had become extremely pale, was at first seized with slight shiverings, horripilations, and tremblings. His pulse was weak and irregular, his skin dry, his thirst intense. To this soon succeeded a hot fit; his face became flushed; his skin reddened; his pulse quick; then a profuse perspiration broke out, after which the fever seemed to diminish. The attack had lasted nearly five hours.

Gideon Spilett had not left Herbert, who, it was only too certain was now seized by an intermittent fever, and this fever must, be cured at any cost before it should assume a more serious aspect.

"And in order to cure it," said Spilett to Cyrus Harding, "we need a febrifuge."

"A febrifuge," answered the engineer. "We have neither Peruvian bark, nor sulphate of quinine?"

"No," said Gideon Spilett, "but there are willows on the border of the lake, and the bark of the willow might, perhaps, prove to be a substitute for quinine."

"Let us try it without losing a moment," replied Cyrus Harding.

The bark of the willow has, indeed, been justly considered as a succedaneum for Peruvian bark, as has also that of the horse-chestnut-tree, the leaf of the holly, the snake-root, etcetera. It was evidently necessary to make trial of this substance, although not so valuable as Peruvian bark, and to employ it in its natural state, since they had no means for extracting its essence.

Cyrus Harding went himself to cut from the trunk of a species of black willow, a few pieces of bark; he brought them back to Granite House, and reduced them to a powder, which was administered that same evening to Herbert.

The night passed without any important change. Herbert was somewhat delirious, but the fever did not reappear in the night, and did not return either during the following day.

Pencroft again began to hope. Gideon Spilett said nothing. It might be that the fever was not quotidian, but tertian, and that it would return next day. Therefore, he awaited the next day with the greatest anxiety.

It might have been remarked besides that during this period Herbert remained utterly prostrate, his head weak and giddy. Another symptom alarmed the reporter to the highest degree. Herbert's liver became congested, and soon a more intense delirium showed that his brain was also affected.

Gideon Spilett was overwhelmed by this new complication. He took the engineer aside.

"It is a malignant fever," said he.

"A malignant fever!" cried Harding. "You are mistaken, Spilett. A malignant fever does not declare itself spontaneously; its germ must previously have existed."

"I am not mistaken," replied the reporter. "Herbert no doubt contracted the germ of this fever in the marshes of the island. He has already had one attack; should a second come on and should we not be able to prevent a third, he is lost."

"But the willow bark?"

"That is insufficient," answered the reporter; "and the third attack of a malignant fever, which is not arrested by means of quinine, is always fatal."

Fortunately, Pencroft heard nothing of this conversation or he would have gone mad.

It may be imagined what anxiety the engineer and the reporter suffered during the day of the 7th of December and the following night.

Towards the middle of the day the second attack came on. The crisis was terrible. Herbert felt himself sinking. He stretched his arms towards Cyrus Harding, towards Spilett, towards Pencroft. He was so young to die! The scene was heartrending. They were obliged to send Pencroft away.

The fit lasted five hours. It was evident that Herbert could not survive a third.

The night was frightful. In his delirium Herbert uttered words which went to the hearts of his companions. He struggled with the convicts, he called to Ayrton, he poured forth entreaties to that mysterious being,—that powerful unknown protector,—whose image was stamped upon his mind; then he again fell into a deep exhaustion which completely prostrated him. Several times Gideon Spilett thought that the poor boy was dead.

The next day, the 8th of December, was but a succession of the fainting fits. Herbert's thin hands clutched the sheets. They had administered further doses of pounded bark, but the reporter expected no result from it.

"If before to-morrow morning we have not given him a more energetic febrifuge," said the reporter, "Herbert will be dead."

Night arrived—the last night, it was too much to be feared, of the good, brave, intelligent boy, so far in advance of his years, and who was loved by all as their own child. The only remedy which existed against this terrible malignant fever, the only specific which could overcome it, was not to be found in Lincoln Island.

During the night of the 8th of December, Herbert was seized by a more violent delirium. His liver was fearfully congested, his brain affected, and already it was impossible for him to recognise any one.

Would he live until the next day, until that third attack which must infallibly carry him off? It was not probable. His strength was exhausted, and in the intervals of fever he lay as one dead.

Towards three o'clock in the morning Herbert uttered a piercing cry. He seemed to be torn by a supreme convulsion. Neb, who was near him, terrified, ran into the next room where his companions were watching.

Top, at that moment, barked in a strange manner.

All rushed in immediately and managed to restrain the dying boy, who was endeavouring to throw himself out of his bed, whilst Spilett, taking his arm, felt his pulse gradually quicken.

It was five in the morning. The rays of the rising sun began to shine in at the windows of Granite House. It promised to be a fine day, and this day was to be poor Herbert's last!

A ray glanced on the table placed near the bed.

Suddenly Pencroft, uttering a cry, pointed to the table.

On it lay a little oblong box, of which the cover bore these words:— "Sulphate of Quinine."

XI

Gideon Spilett took the box and opened it. It contained nearly two hundred grains of a white powder, a few particles of which he carried to his lips. The extreme bitterness of the substance precluded all doubt; it was certainly the precious extract of quinine, that pre-eminent antifebrile.

This powder must be administered to Herbert without delay. How it came there might be discussed later.

"Some coffee!" said Spilett.

In a few moments Neb brought a cup of the warm infusion. Gideon Spilett threw into it about eighteen grains of quinine, and they succeeded in making Herbert drink the mixture.

There was still time, for the third attack of the malignant fever had not yet shown itself. How they longed to be able to add that it would not return!

Besides, it must be remarked, the hopes of all had now revived. The mysterious influence had been again exerted, and in a critical moment, when they had despaired of it.

In a few hours Herbert was much calmer. The colonists could now discuss this incident. The intervention of the stranger was more evident than ever. But how had he been able to penetrate during the night into Granite House? It was inexplicable, and, in truth, the proceedings of the genius of the island were not less mysterious than was that genius himself. During this day the sulphate of quinine was administered to Herbert every three hours.

The next day some improvement in Herbert's condition was apparent. Certainly, he was not out of danger, intermittent fevers being subject to frequent and dangerous relapses, but the most assiduous care was bestowed on him. And besides, the specific was at hand; nor, doubtless, was he who had brought it far-distant! and the hearts of all were animated by returning hope.

This hope was not disappointed. Ten days after, on the 20th of December, Herbert's convalescence commenced.

He was still weak, and strict diet had been imposed upon him, but no access of fever supervened. And then, the poor boy submitted with such docility to all the prescriptions ordered him! He longed so to get well!

Pencroft was as a man who has been drawn up from the bottom of an abyss. Fits of joy approaching to delirium seized him. When the time for the third attack had passed by, he nearly suffocated the reporter in his embrace. Since then, he always called him Dr. Spilett.

The real doctor, however, remained undiscovered.

"We will find him!" repeated the sailor.

Certainly, this man, whoever he was, might expect a somewhat too energetic embrace from the worthy Pencroft!

The month of December ended, and with it the year 1867, during which the colonists of Lincoln Island had of late been so severely tried. They commenced the year 1868 with magnificent weather, great heat, and a tropical temperature, delightfully cooled by the sea-breeze. Herbert's recovery progressed, and from his bed, placed near one of the windows of Granite House, he could inhale the fresh air, charged with ozone, which could not fail to restore his health. His appetite returned, and what numberless delicate, savoury little dishes Neb prepared for him!

"It is enough to make one wish to have a fever oneself!" said Pencroft.

During all this time, the convicts did not once appear in the vicinity of Granite House. There was no news of Ayrton, and though the engineer and Herbert still had some hopes of finding him again, their companions did not doubt but that the unfortunate man had perished. However, this uncertainty could not last, and when once the lad should have recovered, the expedition, the result of which must be so important, would be undertaken. But they would have to wait a month, perhaps, for all the strength of the colony must be put into requisition to obtain satisfaction from the convicts.

However, Herbert's convalescence progressed rapidly. The congestion of the liver had disappeared, and his wounds might be considered completely healed.

During the month of January, important work was done on the plateau of Prospect Heights; but it consisted solely in saving as much as was possible from the devastated crops, either of corn or vegetables.

The grain and the plants were gathered, so as to provide a new harvest for the approaching half-season. With regard to rebuilding the poultry-yard, wall, or stables, Cyrus Harding preferred to wait. Whilst he and his companions were in pursuit of the convicts, the latter might very probably pay another visit to the plateau, and it would be useless to give them an opportunity of recommencing their work of destruction. When the island should be cleared of these miscreants, they would set about rebuilding. The young convalescent began to get up in the second week of January, at first for one hour a day, then two, then three. His strength visibly returned, so vigorous was his constitution. He was now eighteen years of age. He was tall, and promised to become a man of noble and commanding presence. From this time his recovery, while still requiring care,—and Dr. Spilett was very strict,—made rapid; progress. Towards the end of the month, Herbert was already walking about on Prospect Heights, and the beach.

He derived, from several sea-baths, which he took in company with Pencroft and Neb, the greatest possible benefit. Cyrus Harding thought he might now settle the day for their departure, for which the 15th of February was fixed. The nights, very clear at this time of year, would be favourable to the researches they intended to make all over the island.

The necessary preparations for this exploration were now commenced, and were important, for the colonists had sworn not to return to Granite House until their twofold object had been achieved; on the one hand, to exterminate the convicts, and rescue Ayrton, if he was still living; on the other, to discover who it was that presided so effectually over the fortunes of the colony.

Of Lincoln Island, the settlers knew thoroughly all the eastern coast from Claw Cape to the Mandible Capes, the extensive Tadorn Marsh, the neighbourhood of Lake Grant, Jacamar Wood, between the road to the corral and the Mercy, the courses of the Mercy and Red Creek, and lastly, the spurs of Mount Franklin, among which the corral had been established.

They had explored, though only in an imperfect manner, the vast shore of Washington Bay from Claw Cape to Reptile End, the woody and marshy border of the west coast, and the interminable downs, ending at the open mouth of Shark Gulf. But they had in no way surveyed the woods which covered the Serpentine Peninsula, all to the right of the Mercy, the left bank of Falls River, and the wilderness of spurs and valleys which supported three quarters of the base of Mount

Franklin, to the east, the north, and the west, and where doubtless many secret retreats existed. Consequently, many millions of acres of the island had still escaped their investigations.

It was, therefore, decided that the expedition should be carried through the Far West, so as to include all that region situated on the right of the Mercy.

It might, perhaps, be better worth while to go direct to the corral, where it might be supposed that the convicts had again taken refuge, either to pillage or to establish themselves there. But either the devastation of the corral would have been an accomplished fact by this time, and it would be too late to prevent it; or it had been the convicts' interest to intrench themselves there, and there would be still time to go and turn them out on their return.

Therefore, after some discussion, the first plan was adhered to, and the settlers resolved to proceed through the wood to Reptile End. They would make their way with their hatchets, and thus lay the first draft of a road which would place Granite House in communication with the end of the peninsula for a length of from sixteen to seventeen miles.

The cart was in good condition. The onagas, well rested, could go a long journey. Provisions, camp effects, a portable stove, and various utensils were packed in the cart, as also weapons and ammunition, carefully chosen from the now complete arsenal of Granite House. But it was necessary to remember that the convicts were, perhaps, roaming about the woods, and that in the midst of these thick forests a shot might quickly be fired and received. It was therefore resolved that the little band of settlers should remain together and not separate under any pretext whatever.

It was also decided that no one should remain at Granite House. Top and Jup themselves were to accompany the expedition; the inaccessible dwelling needed no guard. The 14th of February, eve of the departure, was Sunday. It was consecrated entirely to repose, and thanksgivings addressed by the colonists to the Creator. A place in the cart was reserved for Herbert, who, though thoroughly convalescent, was still a little weak. The next morning, at daybreak, Cyrus Harding took the necessary measures to protect Granite House from any invasion. The ladders, which were formerly used for the ascent, were brought to the Chimneys and buried deep in the sand, so that they might be available on the return of the colonists, for the machinery of the lift had been taken to pieces, and nothing of the apparatus remained. Pencroft stayed the last in Granite

House in order to finish this work, and he then lowered himself down by means of a double rope held below, and which, when once hauled down, left no communication between the upper landing and the beach.

The weather was magnificent.

"We shall have a warm day of it," said the reporter, laughing.

"Pooh! Dr. Spilett," answered Pencroft, "we shall walk under the shade of the trees and shan't even see the sun!"

"Forward!" said the engineer.

The cart was waiting on the beach before the Chimneys. The reporter made Herbert take his place in it during the first hours at least of the journey, and the lad was obliged to submit to his doctor's orders.

Neb placed himself at the onagas' heads. Cyrus Harding, the reporter, and the sailor, walked in front. Top bounded joyfully along. Herbert offered a seat in his vehicle to Jup, who accepted it without ceremony. The moment for departure had arrived, and the little band set out.

The cart first turned the angle of the mouth of the Mercy, then, having ascended the left bank for a mile, crossed the bridge, at the other side of which commenced the road to Port Balloon and there the explorers, leaving this road on their left, entered the cover of the immense woods which formed the region of the Far West.

For the first two miles the widely-scattered trees allowed the cart to pass with ease; from time to time it became necessary to cut away a few creepers and bushes, but no serious obstacle impeded the progress of the colonists.

The thick foliage of the trees threw a grateful shade on the ground. Deodars, douglas-firs, casuarinas, banksias, gum-trees, dragon-trees, and other well-known species, succeeded each other far as the eye could reach. The feathered tribes of the island were all represented—tetras, jacamars, pheasants, lories, as well as the chattering cockatoos, parrots, and paroquets. Agouties, kangaroos, and capybaras fled swiftly at their approach; and all this reminded the settlers of the first excursions they had made on their arrival at the island.

"Nevertheless," observed Cyrus Harding, "I notice that these creatures, both birds and quadrupeds, are more timid than formerly. These woods have, therefore, been recently traversed by the convicts, and we shall certainly find some traces of them."

And, in fact, in several places they could distinguish traces, more or less recent, of the passage of a band of men—here branches broken off the trees, perhaps to mark out the way; there the ashes of a fire, and footprints in clayey spots; but nothing which appeared to belong to a settled encampment.

The engineer had recommended his companions to refrain from hunting. The reports of the fire-arms might give the alarm to the convicts, who were, perhaps, roaming through the forest. Moreover, the hunters would necessarily ramble some distance from the cart, which it was dangerous to leave unguarded.

In the after-part of the day, when about six miles from Granite House, their progress became much more difficult. In order to make their way through some thickets, they were obliged to cut down trees. Before entering such places Harding was, careful to send in Top and Jup, who faithfully accomplished their commission, and when the dog and orang returned without giving any warning, there was evidently nothing to fear, either from convicts or wild beasts, two varieties of the animal kingdom, whose ferocious instincts placed them on the same level. On the evening of the first day the colonists encamped about nine miles from Granite House, on the border of a little stream falling into the Mercy, and of the existence of which they had till then been ignorant; it evidently, however, belonged to the hydrographical system to which the soil owed its astonishing fertility. The settlers made a hearty meal, for their appetites were sharpened, and measures were then taken that the night might be passed in safety. If the engineer had had only to deal with wild beasts, jaguars, or others, he would have simply lighted fires all round his camp, which would have sufficed for its defence; but the convicts would be rather attracted than terrified by the flames, and it was, therefore, better to be surrounded by the profound darkness of night.

The watch was, however, carefully organised. Two of the settlers were to watch together, and every two hours it was agreed that they should be relieved by their comrades. And so, notwithstanding his wish to the contrary, Herbert was exempted from guard, Pencroft and Gideon Spilett in one party, the engineer and Neb in another, mounted guard in turns over the camp.

The night, however, was but of few hours. The darkness was due rather to the thickness of the foliage than to the disappearance of the sun. The silence was scarcely disturbed by the howling of jaguars and the chattering of the monkeys, the latter appearing to particularly irritate master Jup. The night passed without incident, and on the next day, the 15th of February, the journey through the forest, rather tedious than difficult, was continued. This day they could not accomplish more than six miles, for every moment they were obliged to cut a road with their hatchets.

Like true settlers, the colonists spared the largest and most beautiful trees, which would besides have cost immense labour to fell, and the small ones only were sacrificed, but the result was that the road took a very winding direction, and lengthened itself by numerous *detours*.

During the day Herbert discovered several new specimens not before met with in the island, such as the tree-fern, with its leaves spread out like the waters of a fountain, locust-trees, on the long pods of which the onagas browsed greedily, and which supplied a sweet pulp of excellent flavour. There, too, the colonists again found groups of magnificent kauries, their cylindrical trunks, crowned with a cone of verdure, rising to a height of two hundred feet. These were the tree-kings of New Zealand, as celebrated as the cedars of Lebanon.

As to the fauna, there was no addition to those species already known to the hunters. Nevertheless, they saw, though unable to get near them, a couple of those large birds peculiar to Australia, a sort of cassowary, called emu, five feet in height, and with brown plumage, which belong to the tribe of waders. Top darted after them as fast as his four legs could carry him, but the emus distanced him with ease, so prodigious was their speed.

As to the traces left by the convicts, a few more were discovered. Some footprints found near an apparently recently-extinguished fire were attentively examined by the settlers. By measuring them one after the other, according to their length and breadth, the marks of five men's feet were easily distinguished. The five convicts had evidently camped on this spot; but,—and this was the object of so minute an examination,—a sixth foot-print could not be discovered, which in that case would have been that of Ayrton.

"Ayrton was not with them!" said Herbert.

"No," answered Pencroft, "and if he was not with them, it was because the wretches had already murdered him! but then these rascals have not a den to which they may be tracked like tigers!"

"No," replied the reporter; "it is more probable that they wander at random, and it is their interest to rove about until the time when they will be masters of the island!"

"The masters of the island!" exclaimed the sailor; "the masters of the island!" he repeated, and his voice was choked, as if his throat was seized in an iron grasp. Then in a calmer tone, "Do you know, Captain Harding," said he, "what the ball is which I have rammed into my gun?"

"No, Pencroft!"

"It is the ball that went through Herbert's chest, and I promise you it won't miss its mark!"

But this just retaliation would not bring Ayrton back to life, and from the examination of the footprints left in the ground, they must, alas! conclude that all hopes of ever seeing him again must be abandoned.

That evening they encamped fourteen miles from Granite House, and Cyrus Harding calculated that they could not be more than five miles from Reptile Point.

And, indeed, the next day the extremity of the peninsula was reached, and the whole length of the forest had been traversed; but there was nothing to indicate the retreat in which the convicts had taken refuge, nor that, no less secret, which sheltered the mysterious unknown.

JULES VERNE (TRANSLATION FROM W.H.G. KINGSTON)

XII

EXPLORATION OF THE SERPENTINE PENINSULA—ENCAMPMENT AT
THE MOUTH OF FALLS RIVER—GIDEON SPILETT AND PENCROFT
RECONNOITRE—THEIR RETURN—FORWARD, ALL!—AN OPEN
DOOR—A LIGHTED WINDOW—BY THE LIGHT OF THE MOON!

The next day, the 18th of February, was devoted to the exploration of all that wooded region forming the shore from Reptile End to Falls River. The colonists were able to search this forest thoroughly, for, as it was comprised between the two shores of the Serpentine Peninsula, it was only from three to four miles in breadth. The trees, both by their height and their thick foliage, bore witness to the vegetative power of the soil, more astonishing here than in any other part of the island. One might have said that a corner from the virgin forests of America or Africa had been transported into this temperate zone. This led them to conclude that the superb vegetation found a heat in this soil, damp in its upper layer, but warmed in the interior by volcanic fires, which could not belong to a temperate climate. The most frequently-occurring trees were kauries and eucalypti of gigantic dimensions.

But the colonists' object was not simply to admire the magnificent vegetation. They knew already that in this respect Lincoln Island would have been worthy to take the first rank in the Canary group, to which the first name given was that of the Happy Isles. Now, alas! their island no longer belonged to them entirely; others had taken possession of it, miscreants polluted its shores, and they must be destroyed to the last man.

No traces were found on the western coast, although they were carefully sought for. No more footprints, no more broken branches, no more deserted camps.

"This does not surprise me," said Cyrus Harding to his companions. "The convicts first landed on the island in the neighbourhood of Flotsam Point, and they immediately plunged into the Far West forests, after crossing Tadorn Marsh. They then followed almost the same route that we took on leaving Granite House. This explains the traces we found in the wood. But, arriving on the shore, the convicts saw at once that they would discover no suitable retreat there, and it was then that, going northwards again, they came upon the corral."

"Where they have perhaps returned," said Pencroft.

"I do not think so," answered the engineer, "for they would naturally suppose that our researches would be in that direction. The corral is only a store-house to them, and not a definitive encampment."

"I am of Cyrus' opinion," said the reporter, "and I think that it is among the spurs of Mount Franklin that the convicts will have made their lair."

"Then, captain, straight to the corral!" cried Pencroft. "We must finish them off, and till now we have only lost time!"

"No, my friend," replied the engineer; "you forget that we have a reason for wishing to know if the forests of the Far West do not contain some habitation. Our exploration has a double object, Pencroft. If, on the one hand, we have to chastise crime, we have, on the other, an act of gratitude to perform."

"That was well said, captain," replied the sailor; "but, all the same, it is my opinion that we shall not find that gentleman until he pleases."

And truly Pencroft only expressed the opinion of all. It was probable that the stranger's retreat was not less mysterious than was he himself.

That evening the cart halted at the mouth of Falls River. The camp was organised as usual, and the customary precautions were taken for the night. Herbert, become again the healthy and vigorous lad he was before his illness, derived great benefit from this life in the open air, between the sea-breezes and the vivifying air from the forests. His place was no longer in the cart, but at the head of the troop.

The next day, the 19th of February, the colonists, leaving the shore, where, beyond the mouth, basalts of every shape were so picturesquely piled up, ascended the river by its left bank. The road had been already partially cleared in their former excursions made from the corral to the west coast. The settlers were now about six miles from Mount Franklin.

The engineer's plan was this:—To minutely survey the valley forming the bed of the river, and to cautiously approach the neighbourhood of the corral; if the corral was occupied, to seize it by force; if it was not, to intrench themselves there and make it the centre of the operations which had for their object the exploration of Mount Franklin.

This plan was unanimously approved by the colonists, for they were impatient to regain entire possession of their island.

They made their way along the narrow valley separating two of the largest spurs of Mount Franklin. The trees, crowded on the river's bank, became rare on the upper slopes of the mountain. The ground was hilly and rough, very suitable for ambushes, and over which they did not venture without extreme precaution. Top and Jup skirmished on the flanks, springing right and left through the thick brushwood, and emulating each other in intelligence and activity. But nothing showed that the banks of the stream had been recently frequented— nothing announced either the presence or the proximity of the convicts. Towards five in the evening the cart stopped nearly 600 feet from the palisade. A semicircular screen of trees still hid it.

It was necessary to reconnoitre the corral, in order to ascertain if it was occupied. To go there openly, in broad daylight, when the convicts were probably in ambush, would be to expose themselves, as poor Herbert had done, to the fire-arms of the ruffians. It was better, then, to wait until night came on.

However, Gideon Spilett wished without further delay to reconnoitre the approaches to the corral, and Pencroft, who was quite out of patience, volunteered to accompany him.

"No, my friends," said the engineer, "wait till night. I will not allow one of you to expose himself in open day."

"But, captain," answered the sailor, little disposed to obey.

"I beg you, Pencroft," said the engineer.

"Very well!" replied the sailor, who vented his anger in another way, by bestowing on the convicts the worst names in his maritime vocabulary.

The colonists remained, therefore, near the cart, and carefully watched the neighbouring parts of the forest.

Three hours passed thus. The wind had fallen, and absolute silence reigned under the great trees. The snapping of the smallest twig, a footstep on the dry leaves, the gliding of a body amongst the grass, would have been heard without difficulty. All was quiet. Besides, Top, lying on the grass, his head stretched out on his paws, gave no signs of uneasiness. At eight o'clock the day appeared far enough advanced for the reconnaissance to be made under favourable conditions. Gideon Spilett declared himself ready to set out accompanied by Pencroft. Cyrus Harding consented. Top and Jup were to remain with the engineer, Herbert, and Neb, for a bark or a cry at a wrong moment would give the alarm.

"Do not be imprudent," said Harding to the reporter and Pencroft; "you have not to gain possession of the corral, but only to find out whether it is occupied or not."

"All right," answered Pencroft.

And the two departed.

Under the trees, thanks to the thickness of their foliage, the obscurity rendered any object invisible beyond a radius of from thirty to forty feet. The reporter and Pencroft, halting at any suspicious sound, advanced with great caution.

They walked a little distance apart from each other so as to offer a less mark for a shot. And, to tell the truth, they expected every moment to hear a report. Five minutes after leaving the cart, Gideon Spilett and Pencroft arrived at the edge of the wood before the clearing beyond which rose the palisade.

They stopped. A few straggling beams still fell on the field clear of trees. Thirty feet distant was the gate of the corral, which appeared to be closed. This thirty feet, which it was necessary to cross from the border of the wood to the palisade, constituted the dangerous zone, to coin a term: in fact, one or more bullets fired from behind the palisade might knock over any one who ventured onto this zone. Gideon Spilett and the sailor were not men to draw back, but they knew that any imprudence on their part, of which they would be the first victims, would fall afterwards on their companions. If they themselves were killed, what would become of Harding, Neb, and Herbert?

But Pencroft, excited at feeling himself so near the corral where he supposed the convicts had taken refuge, was about to press forward, when the reporter held him back with a grasp of iron.

"In a few minutes it will be quite dark," whispered Spilett in the sailor's ear; "then will be the time to act."

Pencroft, convulsively clasping the butt-end of his gun, restrained his eagerness, and waited, swearing to himself.

Soon the last of the twilight faded away. Darkness, which seemed as if it issued from the dense forest, covered the clearing. Mount Franklin rose like an enormous screen before the western horizon, and night spread rapidly over all, as it does in regions of low latitudes. Now was the time.

The reporter and Pencroft, since posting themselves on the edge of the wood, had not once lost sight of the palisade. The corral appeared to be absolutely deserted. The top of the palisade formed a line, a little darker than the surrounding shadow, and nothing disturbed its distinctness. Nevertheless, if the convicts were there, they must have posted one of their number to guard against any surprise.

Spilett grasped his companion's hand, and both crept towards the corral, their guns ready to fire.

They reached the gate without the darkness being illuminated by a single ray of light.

Pencroft tried to push open the gate, which, as the reporter and he had supposed, was closed. However, the sailor was able to ascertain that the outer bars had not been put up. It might, then, be concluded that the convicts were there in the corral, and that very probably they had fastened the gate in such a way that it could not be forced open.

Gideon Spilett and Pencroft listened. Not a sound could be heard inside the palisade. The musmons and the goats, sleeping no doubt in their huts, in no way disturbed the calm of night.

The reporter and the sailor hearing nothing, asked themselves whether they had not better scale the palisades and penetrate into the corral. This would have been contrary to Cyrus Harding's instructions.

It is true that the enterprise might succeed, but it might also fail. Now, if the convicts were suspecting nothing, if they knew nothing of the expedition against them, if, lastly, there now existed a chance of surprising them, ought this chance to be lost by inconsiderately attempting to cross the palisade?

This was not the reporter's opinion. He thought it better to wait until all the settlers were collected together before attempting to penetrate into the corral. One thing was certain, that it was possible to reach the palisade without being seen, and also that it did not appear to be guarded. This point settled, there was nothing to be done but to return to the cart, where they would consult.

Pencroft probably agreed with this decision, for he followed the reporter without making any objection when the latter turned back to the wood.

In a few minutes the engineer was made acquainted with the state of affairs.

"Well," said he, after a little thought, "I now have reason to believe that the convicts are not in the corral."

"We shall soon know," said Pencroft, "when we have scaled the palisade."

"To the corral, my friends!" said Cyrus Harding.

"Shall we leave the cart in the wood?" asked Neb.

"No," replied the engineer, "it is our waggon of ammunition and provisions, and, if necessary, it would serve as an intrenchment."

"Forward, then!" said Gideon Spilett.

The cart emerged from the wood and began to roll noiselessly towards the palisade. The darkness was now profound, the silence as complete as when Pencroft and the reporter crept over the ground. The thick grass completely muffled their footsteps.

The colonists held themselves ready to fire. Jup, at Pencroft's orders, kept behind. Neb led Top in a leash, to prevent him from bounding forward.

The clearing soon came in sight. It was deserted. Without hesitating, the little band moved towards the palisade. In a short space of time the dangerous zone was passed. Not a shot had been fired. When the cart reached the palisade, it stopped. Neb remained at the onagas' heads to hold them. The engineer, the reporter, Herbert, and Pencroft, proceeded to the door, in order to ascertain if it was barricaded inside. It was open!

"What do you say now?" asked the engineer, turning to the sailor and Spilett. Both were stupefied.

"I can swear," said Pencroft, "that this gate was shut just now!"

The colonists now hesitated. Were the convicts in the corral when Pencroft and the reporter made their reconnaissance? it could not be doubted, as the gate then closed could only have been opened by them. Were they still there, or had one of their number just gone out?

All these questions presented themselves simultaneously to the minds of the colonists, but how could they be answered?

At that moment, Herbert, who had advanced a few steps into the enclosure, drew back hurriedly, and seized Harding's hand.

"What's the matter?" asked the engineer. "Alight!"

"In the house?"

"Yes!"

All five advanced and indeed, through the window fronting them, they saw glimmering a feeble light. Cyrus Harding made up his mind rapidly. "It is our only chance," said he to his companions, "of finding the convicts collected in this house, suspecting nothing! They are in our power! Forward!" The colonists crossed through the enclosure, holding their guns ready in their hands. The cart had been left outside under the charge of Jup and Top, who had been prudently tied to it.

Cyrus Harding, Pencroft, and Gideon Spilett on one side, Herbert and Neb on the other, going along by the palisade, surveyed the absolutely dark and deserted corral.

In a few moments they were near the closed door of the house.

Harding signed to his companions not to stir, and approached the window, then feebly lighted by the inner light. He gazed into the apartment.

On the table burned a lantern. Near the table was the bed formerly used by Ayrton.

On the bed lay the body of a man.

Suddenly Cyrus Harding drew back, and in a hoarse voice—

"Ayrton!" he exclaimed.

Immediately the door was forced rather than opened, and the colonists rushed into the room.

Ayrton appeared to be asleep. His countenance showed that he had long and cruelly suffered. On his wrists and ankles could be seen great bruises.

Harding bent over him.

"Ayrton!" cried the engineer, seizing the arm of the man whom he had just found again under such unexpected circumstances.

At this exclamation Ayrton opened his eyes, and, gazing at Harding, then at the others—

"You!" he cried, "you?"

"Ayrton! Ayrton!" repeated Harding.

"Where am I?"

"In the house in the corral!"

"Alone?"

"Yes!"

"But they will come back!" cried Ayrton. "Defend yourselves! defend yourselves!"

And he fell back exhausted.

"Spilett," exclaimed the engineer, "we may be attacked at any moment. Bring the cart into the corral. Then barricade the door, and all come back here."

Pencroft, Neb, and the reporter hastened to execute the engineer's orders. There was not a moment to be lost. Perhaps even now the cart was in the hands of the convicts!

In a moment the reporter and his two companions had crossed the corral and reached the gate of the palisade behind which Top was heard growling sullenly.

The engineer, leaving Ayrton for an instant, came out ready to fire. Herbert was at his side. Both surveyed the crest of the spur overlooking the corral. If the convicts were lying in ambush there, they might knock the settlers over one after the other.

At that moment the moon appeared in the east, above the black curtain of the forest, and a white sheet of light spread over the interior of the enclosure. The corral, with its clumps of trees, the little stream which watered it, and its wide carpet of grass, was suddenly illuminated. From the side of the mountain, the house and a part of the palisade stood out white in the moonlight. On the opposite side towards the door, the enclosure remained dark.

A black mass soon appeared. This was the cart entering the circle of light, and Cyrus Harding could hear the noise made by the door, as his companions shut it and fastened the interior bars.

But, at that moment, Top, breaking loose, began to bark furiously and rush to the back of the corral, to the right of the house.

"Be ready to fire, my friends!" cried Harding.

The colonists raised their pieces and waited the moment to fire.

Top still barked, and Jup, running towards the dog, uttered shrill cries.

The colonists followed him, and reached the borders of the little stream, shaded by large trees. And there, in the bright moonlight, what did they see? Five corpses, stretched on the bank!

They were those of the convicts who, four months previously, had landed on Lincoln Island!

XIII

Ayrton's Story—Plans of his former Accomplices—Their
Installation in the Corral—The avenging Justice
of Lincoln Island—The Bonadventure—Researches
around Mount Franklin—The Upper Valleys—
A subterranean Volcano—Pencroft's Opinion—
At the Bottom of the Crater—Return.

How had it happened? Who had killed the convicts? Was it Ayrton? No, for a moment before he was dreading their return.

But Ayrton was now in a profound stupor, from which it was no longer possible to rouse him. After uttering those few words he had again become unconscious, and had fallen back motionless on the bed.

The colonists, a prey to a thousand confused thoughts, under the influence of violent excitement, waited all night, without leaving Ayrton's house, or returning to the spot where lay the bodies of the convicts. It was very probable that Ayrton would not be able to throw any light on the circumstances under which the bodies had been found, since he himself was not aware that he was in the corral. But at any rate he would be in a position to give an account of what had taken place before this terrible execution. The next day Ayrton awoke from his torpor, and his companions cordially manifested all the joy they felt, on seeing him again, almost safe and sound, after a hundred and four days' separation.

Ayrton then in a few words recounted what had happened, or at least as much as he knew.

The day after his arrival at the corral, on the 10th of last November, at nightfall, he was surprised by the convicts, who had scaled the palisade. They bound and gagged him; then he was led to a dark cavern, at the foot of Mount Franklin, where the convicts had taken refuge.

His death had been decided upon, and the next day the convicts were about to kill him, when one of them recognised him, and called him by the name which he bore in Australia. The wretches had no scruples as to murdering Ayrton! They spared Ben Joyce!

But from that moment Ayrton was exposed to the importunities of his former accomplices. They wished him to join them again, and relied upon his aid to enable them to gain possession of Granite House, to penetrate into that hitherto inaccessible dwelling, and to become masters of the island, after murdering the colonists!

Ayrton remained firm. The once convict, now repentant and pardoned, would rather die than betray his companions. Ayrton—bound, gagged, and closely watched—lived in this cave for four months.

Nevertheless the convicts had discovered the corral a short time after their arrival in the island, and since then they had subsisted on Ayrton's stores, but did not live at the corral.

On the 11th of November, two of the villains, surprised by the colonists' arrival, fired at Herbert, and one of them returned, boasting of having killed one of the inhabitants of the island; but he returned alone. His companion, as is known, fell by Cyrus Harding's dagger.

Ayrton's anxiety and despair may be imagined when he learnt the news of Herbert's death. The settlers were now only four, and, as it seemed, at the mercy of the convicts. After this event, and during all the time that the colonists, detained by Herbert's illness, remained in the corral, the pirates did not leave their cavern, and even after they had pillaged the plateau of Prospect Heights, they did not think it prudent to abandon it.

The ill-treatment inflicted on Ayrton was now redoubled. His hands and feet still bore the bloody marks of the cords which bound him day and night. Every moment he expected to be put to death, nor did it appear possible that he could escape.

Matters remained thus until the third week of February. The convicts, still watching for a favourable opportunity, rarely quitted their retreat, and only made a few hunting excursions, either to the interior of the island, or the south coast.

Ayrton had no further news of his friends, and relinquished all hope of ever seeing them again. At last, the unfortunate man, weakened by ill-treatment, fell into a prostration so profound that sight and hearing failed him. From that moment, that is to say, since the last two days, he could give no information whatever of what had occurred.

"But, Captain Harding," he added, "since I was imprisoned in that cavern, how is it that I find myself in the corral?"

"How is it that the convicts are lying yonder dead, in the middle of the enclosure?" answered the engineer.

"Dead!" cried Ayrton, half rising from his bed, notwithstanding his weakness.

His companions supported him. He wished to get up, and with their assistance he did so. They then proceeded together towards the little stream.

It was now broad daylight.

There, on the bank, in the position in which they had been stricken by death in its most instantaneous form, lay the corpses of the five convicts!

Ayrton was astounded. Harding and his companions looked at him without uttering a word. On a sign from the engineer, Neb and Pencroft examined the bodies, already stiffened by the cold.

They bore no apparent trace of any wound.

Only, after carefully examining them, Pencroft found on the forehead of one, on the chest of another, on the back of this one, on the shoulder of that, a little red spot, a sort of scarcely visible bruise, the cause of which it was impossible to conjecture.

"It is there that they have been struck!" said Cyrus Harding.

"But with what weapon?" cried the reporter.

"A weapon, lightning-like in its effects, and of which we have not the secret!"

"And who has struck the blow?" asked Pencroft.

"The avenging power of the island," replied Harding, "he who brought you here, Ayrton, whose influence has once more manifested itself, who does for us all that which we cannot do for ourselves, and who, his will accomplished, conceals himself from us."

"Let us make search for him, then!" exclaimed Pencroft.

"Yes, we will search for him," answered Harding; "but we shall not discover this powerful being who performs such wonders, until he pleases to call us to him!"

This invisible protection, which rendered their own action unavailing, both irritated and piqued the engineer. The relative inferiority which it proved was of a nature to wound a haughty spirit. A generosity evinced in such a manner as to elude all tokens of gratitude, implied a sort of disdain for those on whom the obligation was conferred, which in Cyrus Harding's eyes marred, in some degree, the worth of the benefit.

"Let us search," he resumed, "and God grant that we may some day be permitted to prove to this haughty protector that he has not to deal with ungrateful people! What would I not give could we repay him, by rendering him in our turn, although at the price of our lives, some signal service!"

From this day, the thoughts of the inhabitants of Lincoln Island were solely occupied with the intended search. Everything incited them to discover the answer to this enigma, an answer which could only be the name of a man endowed with a truly inexplicable, and in some degree superhuman power. In a few minutes, the settlers re-entered the house, where their influence soon restored to Ayrton his moral and physical energy.

Neb and Pencroft carried the corpses of the convicts into the forest, some distance from the corral, and buried them deep in the ground.

Ayrton was then made acquainted with the facts which had occurred during his seclusion. He learnt Herbert's adventures, and through what various trials the colonists had passed. As to the settlers, they had despaired of ever seeing Ayrton again, and had been convinced that the convicts had ruthlessly murdered him.

"And now," said Cyrus Harding, as he ended his recital, "a duty remains for us to perform. Half of our task is accomplished, but although the convicts are no longer to be feared, it is not owing to ourselves that we are once more masters of the island."

"Well!" answered Gideon Spilett, "let us search all this labyrinth of the spurs of Mount Franklin. We will not leave a hollow, not a hole unexplored! Ah! if ever a reporter found himself face to face with a mystery, it is I who now speak to you, my friends!"

"And we will not return to Granite House until we have found our benefactor," said Herbert.

"Yes," said the engineer, "we will do all that it is humanly possible to do, but I repeat we shall not find him until he himself permits us."

"Shall we stay at the corral?" asked Pencroft.

"We shall stay here," answered Harding. "Provisions are abundant, and we are here in the very centre of the circle we have to explore. Besides, if necessary, the cart will take us rapidly to Granite House."

"Good!" answered the sailor. "Only I have a remark to make."

"What is it?"

"Here is the fine season getting on, and we must not forget that we have a voyage to make."

"A voyage?" said Gideon Spilett.

"Yes, to Tabor Island," answered Pencroft. "It is necessary to carry a notice there to point out the position of our island and say that Ayrton is here in case the Scotch yacht should come to take him off. Who knows if it is not already too late?"

"But, Pencroft," asked Ayrton, "how do you intend to make this voyage?"

"In the *Bonadventure*."

"The *Bonadventure*!" exclaimed Ayrton. "She no longer exists."

"My *Bonadventure* exists no longer!" shouted Pencroft, bounding from his seat.

"No," answered Ayrton. "The convicts discovered her in her little harbour only eight days ago, they put to sea in her, and—"

"And?" said Pencroft, his heart beating.

"And not having Bob Harvey to steer her, they ran on the rocks, and the vessel went to pieces."

"Oh, the villains, the cut-throats, the infamous scoundrels!" exclaimed Pencroft.

"Pencroft," said Herbert, taking the sailor's hand, "we will build another *Bonadventure*—a larger one. We have all the iron-work—all the rigging of the brig at our disposal."

"But do you know," returned Pencroft, "that it will take at least five or six months to build a vessel of from thirty to forty tons?"

"We can take our time," said the reporter, "and we must give up the voyage to Tabor Island for this year."

"Oh, my *Bonadventure*! my poor *Bonadventure*!" cried Pencroft, almost broken-hearted at the destruction of the vessel of which he was so proud.

The loss of the *Bonadventure* was certainly a thing to be lamented by the colonists, and it was agreed that this loss should be repaired as soon as possible. This settled, they now occupied themselves with bringing their researches to bear on the most secret parts of the island.

The exploration was commenced at daybreak on the 19th of February, and lasted an entire week. The base of the mountain, with its spurs and their numberless ramifications, formed a labyrinth of valleys and elevations. It was evident that there, in the depths of these narrow gorges, perhaps even in the interior of Mount Franklin itself, was the proper place to pursue their researches. No part of the island could have been more suitable to conceal a dwelling whose occupant wished to remain unknown. But so irregular was the formation of the valleys that Cyrus Harding was obliged to conduct the exploration in a strictly methodical manner.

The colonists first visited the valley opening to the south of the volcano, and which first received the waters of Falls River. There Ayrton showed them the cavern where the convicts had taken refuge, and in which he had been imprisoned until his removal to the corral. This cavern was just as Ayrton had left it. They found there a considerable quantity of ammunition and provisions, conveyed thither by the convicts in order to form a reserve.

The whole of the valley bordering on the cave, shaded by fir and other trees, was thoroughly explored, and on turning the point of the south-western spur, the colonists entered a narrower gorge similar to the picturesque columns of basalt on the coast. Here the trees were fewer. Stones took the place of grass. Goats and musmons gambolled among the rocks. Here began the barren part of the island. It could already be seen that, of the numerous valleys branching off at the base of Mount Franklin, three only were wooded and rich in pasturage like that of the corral, which bordered on the west on the Falls River valley, and on the east on the Red Creek valley. These two streams, which lower down became rivers by the absorption of several tributaries, were formed by all the springs of the mountain and thus caused the fertility of its southern part. As to the Mercy, it was more directly fed from ample springs concealed under the cover of Jacamar Wood, and it was by springs of this nature, spreading in a thousand streamlets, that the soil of the Serpentine Peninsula was watered.

Now, of these three well-watered valleys, either might have served as a retreat to some solitary who would have found there everything necessary for life. But the settlers had already explored them, and in no part had they discovered the presence of man.

Was it then in the depths of those barren gorges, in the midst of the piles of rock, in the rugged northern ravines, among the streams of lava, that this dwelling and its occupant would be found?

The northern part of Mount Franklin was at its base composed solely of two valleys, wide, not very deep, without any appearance of vegetation, strewn with masses of rock, paved with lava, and varied with great blocks of mineral. This region required a long and careful exploration. It contained a thousand cavities, comfortless no doubt, but perfectly concealed and difficult of access.

The colonists even visited dark tunnels, dating from the volcanic period, still black from the passage of the fire, and penetrated into the depths of the mountain. They traversed these sombre galleries, waving lighted torches; they examined the smallest excavations; they sounded the shallowest depths, but all was dark and silent. It did not appear that the foot of man had ever before trodden these ancient passages, or that his arm had ever displaced one of these blocks, which remained as the volcano had cast them up above the waters, at the time of the submersion of the island.

However, although these passages appeared to be absolutely deserted, and the obscurity was complete, Cyrus Harding was obliged to confess that absolute silence did not reign there.

On arriving at the end of one of these gloomy caverns, extending several hundred feet into the interior of the mountain, he was surprised to hear a deep rumbling noise, increased in intensity by the sonorousness of the rocks.

Gideon Spilett, who accompanied him, also heard these distant mutterings, which indicated a revivification of the subterranean fires. Several times both listened, and they agreed that some chemical process was taking place in the bowels of the earth.

"Then the volcano is not totally extinct?" said the reporter.

"It is possible that since our exploration of the crater," replied Cyrus Harding, "some change has occurred. Any volcano, although considered extinct, may evidently again burst forth."

"But if an eruption of Mount Franklin occurred," asked Spilett, "would there not be some danger to Lincoln Island?"

"I do not think so," answered the reporter. "The crater—that is to say, the safety-valve, exists, and the overflow of smoke and lava would escape, as it did formerly, by its customary outlet."

"Unless the lava opened a new way for itself towards the fertile parts of the island!"

"And why, my dear Spilett," answered Cyrus Harding, "should it not follow the road naturally traced out for it?"

"Well, volcanoes are capricious," returned the reporter.

"Notice," answered the engineer, "that the inclination of Mount Franklin favours the flow of water towards the valleys which we are exploring just now. To turn aside this flow, an earthquake would be necessary to change the mountain's centre of gravity."

"But an earthquake is always to be feared at these times," observed Gideon Spilett.

"Always," replied the engineer, "especially when the subterranean forces begin to awake, as they risk meeting with some obstruction, after a long rest. Thus, my dear Spilett, an eruption would be a serious thing for us, and it would be better that the volcano should not have the slightest desire to wake up. But we could not prevent it, could we? At any rate, even if it should occur, I do not think Prospect Heights would be seriously threatened. Between them and the mountain, the ground is considerably depressed, and if the lava should ever take a course towards the lake, it would be cast on the downs and the neighbouring parts of Shark Gulf."

"We have not yet seen any smoke at the top of the mountain, to indicate an approaching eruption," said Gideon Spilett.

"No," answered Harding, "not a vapour escapes from the crater, for it was only yesterday that I attentively surveyed the summit. But it is probable that at the lower part of the chimney, time may have accumulated rocks, cinders, hardened lava, and that this valve of which I spoke, may at any time become overcharged. But at the first serious effort, every obstacle will disappear, and you may be certain, my dear Spilett, that neither the island, which is the boiler, nor the volcano, which is the chimney, will burst under the pressure of gas. Nevertheless, I repeat, it would be better that there should not be an eruption."

"And yet we are not mistaken," remarked the reporter. "Mutterings can be distinctly heard in the very bowels of the volcano!"

"You are right," said the engineer, again listening attentively. "There can be no doubt of it. A commotion is going on there, of which we can neither estimate the importance nor the ultimate result."

Cyrus Harding and Spilett, on coming out, rejoined their companions, to whom they made known the state of affairs.

"Very well!" cried Pencroft, "the volcano wants to play his pranks! Let him try, if he likes! He will find his master!"

"Who?" asked Neb.

"Our good genius, Neb, our good genius, who will shut his mouth for him, if he so much as pretends to open it!"

As may be seen, the sailor's confidence in the tutelary deity of his island was absolute, and, certainly, the occult power, manifested until now in so many inexplicable ways, appeared to be unlimited; but also it knew how to escape the colonists' most minute researches, for, in spite of all their efforts, in spite of the more than zeal,—the obstinacy,—with which they carried on their exploration, the retreat of the mysterious being could not be discovered.

From the 19th to the 25th of February the circle of investigation was extended to all the northern region of Lincoln Island, whose most secret nooks were explored. The colonists even went the length of tapping every rock. The search was extended to the extreme verge of the mountain. It was explored thus to the very summit of the truncated cone terminating the first row of rocks, then to the upper ridge of the enormous hat, at the bottom of which opened the crater.

They did more; they visited the gulf, now extinct, but in whose depths the rumbling could be distinctly heard. However, no sign of smoke or vapour, no heating of the rock, indicated an approaching eruption. But neither there, nor in any other part of Mount Franklin, did the colonists find any traces of him of whom they were in search.

Their investigations were then directed to the downs. They carefully examined the high lava-cliffs of Shark Gulf from the base to the crest, although it was extremely difficult to reach even the level of the gulf. No one!—nothing!

In short, in these two words was summed up so much fatigue uselessly expended, so much energy producing no result, that somewhat of anger mingled with the discomfiture of Cyrus Harding and his companions.

It was now time to think of returning, for these researches could not be prolonged indefinitely. The colonists were certainly right in believing that the mysterious being did not reside on the surface of the island, and the wildest fancies haunted their excited imaginations. Pencroft and Neb, particularly, were not contented with the mystery, but allowed their imaginations to wander into the domain of the supernatural.

On the 25th of February the colonists re-entered Granite House, and by means of the double cord, carried by an arrow to the threshold of the door, they re-established communication between their habitation and the ground.

A month later they commemorated, on the 25th of March, the third anniversary of their arrival on Lincoln Island.

XIV

Three Years have passed—The new Vessel—
What is agreed on—Prosperity of the Colony—
The Dockyard—Cold of the Southern Hemisphere—
Washing Linen—Mount Franklin.

Three years had passed away since the escape of the prisoners from Richmond, and how often during those three years had they spoken of their country, always present in their thoughts!

They had no doubt that the civil war was at an end, and to them it appeared impossible that the just cause of the North had not triumphed. But what had been the incidents of this terrible war? How much blood had it not cost? How many of their friends must have fallen in the struggle? They often spoke of these things, without as yet being able to foresee the day when they would be permitted once more to see their country. To return thither, were it but for a few days, to renew the social link with the inhabited world, to establish a communication between their native land and their island, then to pass the longest, perhaps the best, portion of their existence in this colony founded by them, and which would then be dependent of their country, was this a dream impossible to realise?

There were only two ways of accomplishing it—either a ship must appear off Lincoln Island, or the colonists must themselves build a vessel strong enough to sail to the nearest land.

"Unless," said Pencroft, "our good genius himself provides us with the means of returning to our country."

And, really, had any one told Pencroft and Neb that a ship of 300 tons was waiting for them in Shark Gulf or at Port Balloon, they would not even have made a gesture of surprise. In their state of mind nothing appeared improbable.

But Cyrus Harding, less confident, advised them to confine themselves to fact, and more especially so with regard to the building of a vessel—a really urgent work, since it was for the purpose of depositing, as soon as possible, at Tabor Island a document indicating Ayrton's new residence.

As the *Bonadventure* no longer existed, six months at least would be required for the construction of a new vessel. Now winter was approaching, and the voyage could not be made before the following spring.

"We have time to get everything ready for the fine season," remarked the engineer, who was consulting with Pencroft about these matters. "I think, therefore, my friend, that since we have to rebuild our vessel it will be best to give her larger dimensions. The arrival of the Scotch yacht at Tabor Island is very uncertain. It may even be that, having arrived several months ago, she has again sailed after having vainly searched for some trace of Ayrton. Will it not then be best to build a ship which, if necessary, could take us either to the Polynesian Archipelago or to New Zealand? What do you think?"

"I think, captain," answered the sailor; "I think that you are as capable of building a large vessel as a small one. Neither the wood nor the tools are wanting. It is only a question of time."

"And how many months would be required to build a vessel of from 250 to 300 tons?" asked Harding.

"Seven or eight months at least," replied Pencroft. "But it must not be forgotten that winter is drawing near, and that in severe frost wood is difficult to work. We must calculate on several weeks' delay, and if our vessel is ready by next November we may think ourselves very lucky."

"Well," replied Cyrus Harding, "that will be exactly the most favourable time for undertaking a voyage of any importance, either to Tabor Island or to a more distant land."

"So it will, captain," answered the sailor. "Make out your plans then; the workmen are ready, and I imagine that Ayrton can lend us a good helping hand."

The colonists, having been consulted, approved the engineer's plan, and it was, indeed, the best thing to be done. It is true that the construction of a ship of from two to three hundred tons would be great labour, but the colonists had confidence in themselves, justified by their previous success.

Cyrus Harding then busied himself in drawing the plan of the vessel and making the model. During this time his companions employed themselves in felling and carting trees to furnish the ribs, timbers, and planks. The forest of the Far West supplied the best oaks and elms. They took advantage of the opening already made on their last excursion to form a practicable road, which they named the Far West Road, and the trees were carried to the Chimneys, where the dockyard was established. As to the road in question, the choice of trees had rendered its direction somewhat capricious, but that at the same time facilitated the access to a large part of the Serpentine Peninsula.

It was important that the trees should be quickly felled and cut up, for they could not be used while yet green, and some time was necessary to allow them to get seasoned. The carpenters, therefore, worked vigorously during the month of April, which was troubled only by a few equinoctial gales of some violence. Master Jup aided them dexterously, either by climbing to the top of a tree to fasten the ropes or by lending his stout shoulders to carry the lopped trunks.

All this timber was piled up under a large shed, built near the Chimneys, and there awaited the time for use.

The month of April was tolerably fine, as October often is in the northern zone. At the same time other work was actively continued, and soon all trace of devastation disappeared from the plateau of Prospect Heights. The mill was rebuilt, and new buildings rose in the poultry-yard. It had appeared necessary to enlarge their dimensions, for the feathered population had increased considerably. The stable now contained five onagas, four of which were well broken, and allowed themselves to be either driven or ridden, and a little colt. The colony now possessed a plough, to which the onagas were yoked like regular Yorkshire or Kentucky oxen. The colonists divided their work, and their arms never tired. Then who could have enjoyed better health than these workers, and what good humour enlivened the evenings in Granite House as they formed a thousand plans for the future!

As a matter of course Ayrton shared the common lot in every respect, and there was no longer any talk of his going to live at the corral. Nevertheless he was still sad and reserved, and joined more in the work than in the pleasures of his companions. But he was a valuable workman at need—strong, skilful, ingenious, intelligent. He was esteemed and loved by all, and he could not be ignorant of it.

In the meanwhile the corral was not abandoned. Every other day one of the settlers, driving the cart or mounted on an onaga, went to look after the flock of musmons and goats and bring back the supply of milk required by Neb. These excursions at the same time afforded opportunities for hunting. Therefore Herbert and Gideon Spilett, with Top in front, traversed more often than their companions the road to the corral, and with the capital guns which they carried, capybaras, agouties, kangaroos, and wild pigs for large game, ducks, tetras, grouse, jacamars, and snipe for small, were never wanting in the house. The produce of the warren, of the oyster-bed, several turtles which were taken, excellent salmon which came up the Mercy, vegetables from the plateau, wild fruit from the forest, were riches upon riches, and Neb, the head cook, could scarcely by himself store them away.

The telegraphic wire between the corral and Granite House had of course been repaired, and it was worked whenever one or other of the settlers was at the corral and found it necessary to spend the night there. Besides, the island was safe now and no attacks were to be feared, at any rate from men.

However, that which had happened might happen again. A descent of pirates, or even of escaped convicts, was always to be feared. It was possible that companions or accomplices of Bob Harvey had been in the secret of his plans, and might be tempted to imitate him. The colonists, therefore, were careful to observe the sea around the island, and every day their telescope swept the horizon enclosed by the Union and Washington Bays. When they went to the corral they examined the sea to the west with no less attention, and by climbing the spur their gaze extended over a large section of the western horizon.

Nothing suspicious was discerned, but still it was necessary for them to be on their guard.

The engineer one evening imparted to his friends a plan which he had conceived for fortifying the corral. It appeared prudent to him to heighten the palisade and to flank it with a sort of block-house, which, if necessary, the settlers could hold against the enemy. Granite House might, by its very position, be considered impregnable; therefore the corral with its buildings, its stores, and the animals it contained, would always be the object of pirates, whoever they were, who might land on the island, and should the colonists be obliged to shut themselves up there they ought also to be able to defend themselves without any disadvantage. This was a project which might be left for consideration, and they were, besides, obliged to put off its execution until the next spring.

About the 15th of May the keel of the new vessel lay along the dockyard, and soon the stem and stern-post, mortised at each of its extremities, rose almost perpendicularly. The keel, of good oak, measured 110 feet in length, this allowing a width of five-and-twenty feet to the midship beam. But this was all the carpenters could do before the arrival of the frosts and bad weather. During the following week they fixed the first of the stern timbers, but were then obliged to suspend work.

During the last days of the month the weather was extremely bad. The wind blew from the east, sometimes with the violence of a tempest. The engineer was somewhat uneasy on account of the dockyard sheds—which, besides, he could not have established in any other place near to Granite House—for the islet only imperfectly sheltered the shore from the fury of the open sea, and in great storms the waves beat against the very foot of the granite cliff.

But, very fortunately, these fears were not realised. The wind shifted to the south-east, and there the beach of Granite House was completely covered by Flotsam Point.

Pencroft and Ayrton, the most zealous workmen at the new vessel, pursued their labour as long as they could. They were not men to mind the wind tearing at their hair, nor the rain wetting them to the skin, and a blow from a hammer is worth just as much in bad as in fine weather. But when a severe frost succeeded this wet period, the wood, its fibres acquiring the hardness of iron, became extremely difficult to work, and about the 10th of June ship-building was obliged to be entirely discontinued.

Cyrus Harding and his companions had not omitted to observe how severe was the temperature during the winters of Lincoln Island. The cold was comparable to that experienced in the States of New England, situated at almost the same distance from the equator. In the northern hemisphere, or at any rate in the part occupied by British America and the north of the United States, this phenomenon is explained by the flat conformation of the territories bordering on the pole, and on which there is no intumescence of the soil to oppose any obstacle to the north winds; here, in Lincoln Island, this explanation would not suffice.

"It has even been observed," remarked Harding one day to his companions, "that in equal latitudes the islands and coast regions are less tried by the cold than inland countries. I have often heard it asserted that the winters of Lombardy, for example, are not less rigorous than those of Scotland, which results from the sea restoring during the winter the heat which it received during the summer. Islands are, therefore, in a better situation for benefiting by this restitution."

"But then, Captain Harding," asked Herbert, "why does Lincoln Island appear to escape the common law?"

"That is difficult to explain," answered the engineer. "However, I should be disposed to conjecture that this peculiarity results from the situation of the island in the southern hemisphere, which, as you know, my boy, is colder than the northern hemisphere."

"Yes," said Herbert, "and icebergs are met with in lower latitudes in the south than in the north of the Pacific."

"That is true," remarked Pencroft, "and when I have been serving on board whalers I have seen icebergs off Cape Horn."

"The severe cold experienced in Lincoln Island," said Gideon Spilett, "may then perhaps be explained by the presence of floes or icebergs comparatively near to Lincoln Island."

"Your opinion is very admissible indeed, my dear Spilett," answered Cyrus Harding, "and it is evidently to the proximity of icebergs that we owe our rigorous winters. I would draw your attention also to an entirely physical cause, which renders the southern colder than the northern hemisphere. In fact, since the sun is nearer to this hemisphere during the summer, it is necessarily more distant during the winter. This explains then the excess of temperature in the two seasons, for, if we find the winters very cold in Lincoln Island, we must not forget that the summers here, on the contrary, are very hot."

"But why, if you please, captain," asked Pencroft, knitting his brows, "why should our hemisphere, as you say, be so badly divided? It isn't just, that!"

"Friend Pencroft," answered the engineer, laughing, "whether just or not, we must submit to it, and here lies the reason for this peculiarity. The earth does not describe a circle round the sun, but an ellipse, as it must by the laws of rational mechanics. Now, the earth occupies one of the centres of the ellipse, and consequently, at the time of its transfer, it is further from the sun, that is to say, at its apogee, and at another time nearer, that is to say, at its perigee. Now it happens that it is during the winter of the southern countries that it is at its most distant point from the sun, and consequently, in a situation for those regions to feel the greatest cold. Nothing can be done to prevent that, and men, Pencroft, however learned they may be, can never change anything of the cosmographical order established by God Himself."

"And yet," added Pencroft, persisting, "the world is very learned. What a big book, captain, might be made with all that is known!"

"And what a much bigger book still with all that is not known!" answered Harding.

At last, for one reason or another, the month of June brought the cold with its accustomed intensity, and the settlers were often confined to Granite House. Ah! how wearisome this imprisonment was to them, and more particularly to Gideon Spilett.

"Look here," said he to Neb one day, "I would give you by notarial deed all the estates which will come to me some day, if you were a good-enough fellow to go, no matter where, and subscribe to some newspaper for me! Decidedly the thing that is most essential to my happiness is the knowing every morning what has happened the day before in other places than this!"

Neb began to laugh.

"'Pon my word," he replied, "the only thing I think about is my daily work!"

The truth was that indoors as well as out there was no want of work.

The colony of Lincoln Island was now at its highest point of prosperity, achieved by three years of continued hard work. The destruction of the brig had been a new source of riches. Without speaking of the complete rig which would serve for the vessel now on the stocks, utensils and tools of all sorts, weapons and ammunition, clothes and instruments, were now piled in the store-rooms of Granite House. It had not even been necessary to resort again to the manufacture of the coarse felt materials. Though the colonists had suffered from cold during their first winter, the bad season might now come without their having any reason to dread its severity. Linen was plentiful also, and besides, they kept it with extreme care. From chloride of sodium, which is nothing else than sea salt, Cyrus Harding easily extracted the soda and chlorine. The soda, which it was easy to change into carbonate of soda, and the chlorine, of which he made chloride of lime, were employed for various domestic purposes, and especially in bleaching linen. Besides, they did not wash more than four times a year, as was done by families in the olden time, and it may be added, that Pencroft and Gideon Spilett, whilst waiting for the postman to bring him his newspaper, distinguished themselves as washermen.

So passed the winter months, June, July, and August. They were very severe, and the average observations of the thermometer did not give more than eight degrees of Fahrenheit. It was therefore lower in temperature than the preceding winter. But then, what splendid fires blazed continually on the hearths of Granite House, the smoke marking the granite wall with long, zebra-like streaks! Fuel was not spared, as it grew naturally a few steps from them. Besides, the chips of the wood destined for the construction of the ship enabled them to economise the coal, which required more trouble to transport.

Men and animals were all well. Master Jup was a little chilly, it must be confessed. This was perhaps his only weakness, and it was necessary to make him a well-wadded dressing-gown. But what a servant he was, clever, zealous, indefatigable, not indiscreet, not talkative, and he might have been with reason proposed as a model for all his biped brothers in the Old and the New World!

"As for that," said Pencroft, "when one has four hands at one's service, of course one's work ought to be done so much the better!"

And indeed the intelligent creature did it well.

During the seven months which had passed since the last researches made round the mountain, and during the month of September, which brought back fine weather, nothing was heard of the genius of the island. His power was not manifested in any way. It is true that it would have been inutile, for no incident occurred to put the colonists to any painful trial.

Cyrus Harding even observed that if by chance the communication between the unknown and the tenants of Granite House had ever been established through the granite, and if Top's instinct had as it were felt it, there was no further sign of it during this period. The dog's growling had entirely ceased, as well as the uneasiness of the orang. The two friends—for they were so—no longer prowled round the opening of the inner well, nor did they bark or whine in that singular way which from the first the engineer had noticed. But could he be sure that this was all that was to be said about this enigma, and that he should never arrive at a solution? Could he be certain that some conjuncture would not occur which would bring the mysterious personage on the scene? Who could tell what the future might have in reserve?

At last the winter was ended, but an event, the consequences of which might be serious, occurred in the first days of the returning spring.

On the 7th of September, Cyrus Harding, having observed the crater, saw smoke curling round the summit of the mountain, its first vapours rising in the air.

XV

THE AWAKENING OF THE VOLCANO—THE FINE SEASON—
CONTINUATION OF WORK—THE EVENING OF THE 15TH OF
OCTOBER—A TELEGRAM—A QUESTION—AN ANSWER—
DEPARTURE FOR THE CORRAL—THE NOTICE—
THE ADDITIONAL WIRE—THE BASALT COAST—AT HIGH
TIDE—AT LOW TIDE—THE CAVERN—A DAZZLING LIGHT.

The colonists, warned by the engineer, left their work and gazed in silence at the summit of Mount Franklin.

The volcano had awoke, and the vapour had penetrated the mineral layer heaped up at the bottom of the crater. But would the subterranean fires provoke any violent eruption? This was an event which could not be foreseen. However, even while admitting the possibility of an eruption, it was not probable that the whole of Lincoln Island would suffer from it. The flow of volcanic matter is not always disastrous, and the island had already undergone this trial, as was shown by the streams of lava hardened on the northern slopes of the mountain. Besides, from the shape of the crater—the opening broken in the upper edge—the matter would be thrown to the side opposite the fertile regions of the island.

However, the past did not necessarily answer for the future. Often, at the summit of volcanoes, the old craters close and new ones open. This has occurred in the two hemispheres—at Etna, Popocatepetl, at Orizaba—and on the eve of an eruption there is everything to be feared. In fact, an earthquake—a phenomenon which often accompanies volcanic eruptions—is enough to change the interior arrangement of a mountain, and to open new outlets for the burning lava.

Cyrus Harding explained these things to his companions, and, without exaggerating the state of things, he told them all the pros and cons. After all they could not prevent it. It did not appear likely that Granite House would be threatened unless the ground was shaken by an earthquake. But the corral would be in great danger should a new crater open in the southern side of Mount Franklin.

From that day the smoke never disappeared from the top of the mountain, and it could even be perceived that it increased in height and thickness, without any flame mingling in its heavy volumes. The phenomenon was still concentrated in the lower part of the central crater.

However, with the fine days work had been continued. The building of the vessel was hastened as much as possible, and, by means of the waterfall on the shore, Cyrus Harding managed to establish an hydraulic saw-mill, which rapidly cut up the trunks of trees into planks and joists. The mechanism of this apparatus was as simple as those used in the rustic saw-mills of Norway. A first horizontal movement to move the piece of wood, a second vertical movement to move the saw—this was all that was wanted; and the engineer succeeded by means of a wheel, two cylinders, and pulleys properly arranged. Towards the end of the month of September the skeleton of the vessel, which was to be rigged as a schooner, lay in the dockyard. The ribs were almost entirely completed, and, all the timbers having been sustained by a provisional band, the shape of the vessel could already be seen. This schooner, sharp in the bows, very slender in the after-part, would evidently be suitable for a long voyage, if wanted; but laying the planking would still take a considerable time. Very fortunately, the iron-work of the pirate brig had been saved after the explosion. From the planks and injured ribs Pencroft and Ayrton had extracted the bolts and a large quantity of copper nails. It was so much work saved for the smiths, but the carpenters had much to do.

Ship-building was interrupted for a week for the harvest, the haymaking, and the gathering in of the different crops on the plateau. This work finished, every moment was devoted to finishing the schooner. When night came the workmen were really quite exhausted. So as not to lose any time they had changed the hours for their meals; they dined at twelve o'clock, and only had their supper when daylight failed them. They then ascended to Granite House, when they were always ready to go to bed.

Sometimes, however, when the conversation bore on some interesting subject the hour for sleep was delayed for a time. The colonists then spoke of the future, and talked willingly of the changes which a voyage in the schooner to inhabited lands would make in their situation. But always, in the midst of these plans, prevailed the thought of a subsequent return to Lincoln Island. Never would they abandon this colony, founded with so much labour and with such success, and to which a communication with America would afford a fresh impetus. Pencroft and Neb especially hoped to end their days there.

"Herbert," said the sailor, "you will never abandon Lincoln Island?"

"Never, Pencroft, and especially if you make up your mind to stay there."

"That was made up long ago, my boy," answered Pencroft. "I shall expect you. You will bring me your wife and children, and I shall make jolly little chaps of your youngsters!"

"That's agreed," replied Herbert, laughing and blushing at the same time.

"And you, Captain Harding," resumed Pencroft enthusiastically, "you will be still the governor of the island! Ah! how many inhabitants could it support? Ten thousand at least!"

They talked in this way, allowing Pencroft to run on, and at last the reporter actually started a newspaper—the *New Lincoln Herald*!

So is man's heart. The desire to perform a work which will endure, which will survive him, is the origin of his superiority over all other living creatures here below. It is this which has established his dominion, and this it is which justifies it, over all the world.

After that, who knows if Jup and Top had not themselves their little dream of the future.

Ayrton silently said to himself that he would like to see Lord Glenarvan again and show himself to all restored.

One evening, on the 15th of October, the conversation was prolonged later than usual. It was nine o'clock. Already, long badly-concealed yawns gave warning of the hour of rest, and Pencroft was proceeding towards his bed, when the electric bell, placed in the dining-room, suddenly rang.

All were there, Cyrus Harding, Gideon Spilett, Herbert, Ayrton, Pencroft, Neb. Therefore none of the colonists were at the corral.

Cyrus Harding rose. His companions stared at each other, scarcely believing their ears.

"What does that mean?" cried Neb. "Was it the devil who rang it?"

No one answered.

"The weather is stormy," observed Herbert. "Might not its influence of electricity—"

Herbert did not finish his phrase. The engineer, towards whom all eyes were turned, shook his head negatively.

"We must wait," said Gideon Spilett. "If it is a signal, whoever it may be who has made it, he will renew it."

"But who do you think it is?" cried Neb. "Who?" answered Pencroft, "but he—"

The sailor's sentence was cut short by a new tinkle of the bell.

Harding went to the apparatus, and sent this question to the corral:—

"What do you want?"

A few moments later the needle, moving on the alphabetic dial, gave this reply to the tenants of Granite House:—

"Come to the corral immediately."

"At last!" exclaimed Harding.

Yes! At last! The mystery was about to be unveiled. The colonists' fatigue had disappeared before the tremendous interest which was about to urge them to the corral, and all wish for rest had ceased. Without having uttered a word, in a few moments they had left Granite House, and were standing on the beach. Jup and Top alone were left behind. They could do without them.

The night was black. The new moon had disappeared at the same time as the sun. As Herbert had observed great stormy clouds formed a lowering and heavy vault, preventing any star rays. A few lightning-flashes, reflections from a distant storm, illuminated the horizon.

It was possible that a few hours later the thunder would roll over the island itself. The night was very threatening. But however deep the darkness was, it would not prevent them from finding the familiar road to the corral.

They ascended the left bank of the Mercy, reached the plateau, passed the bridge over Creek Glycerine, and advanced through the forest.

They walked at a good pace, a prey to the liveliest emotions. There was no doubt but that they were now going to learn the long-searched-for answer to the enigma, the name of that mysterious being, so deeply concerned in their life, so generous in his influence, so powerful in his action! Must not this stranger have indeed mingled with their existence, have known the smallest details, have heard all that was said in Granite House, to have been able always to act in the very nick of time?

Every one, wrapped up in his own reflections, pressed forward. Under the arch of trees the darkness was such that the edge of the road even could not be seen. Not a sound in the forest. Both animals and birds, influenced by the heaviness of the atmosphere, remained motionless and silent. Not a breath disturbed the leaves. The footsteps of the colonists alone resounded on the hardened ground.

During the first quarter of an hour the silence was only interrupted by this remark from Pencroft:—

"We ought to have brought a torch."

And by this reply from the engineer:—

"We shall find one at the corral."

Harding and his companions had left Granite House at twelve minutes past nine. At forty-seven minutes past nine they had traversed three out of the five miles which separated the mouth of the Mercy from the corral.

At that moment sheets of lightning spread over the island and illumined the dark trees. The flashes dazzled and almost blinded them. Evidently the storm would not be long in bursting forth.

The flashes gradually became brighter and more rapid. Distant thunder growled in the sky. The atmosphere was stifling.

The colonists proceeded as if they were urged onwards by some irresistible force.

At ten o'clock a vivid flash showed them the palisade, and as they reached the gate the storm burst forth with tremendous fury.

In a minute the corral was crossed, and Harding stood before the hut.

Probably the house was occupied by the stranger, since it was from thence that the telegram had been sent. However, no light shone through the window.

The engineer knocked at the door.

No answer.

Cyrus Harding opened the door, and the settlers entered the room, which was perfectly dark. A light was struck by Neb, and in a few moments the lantern was lighted and the light thrown into every corner of the room.

There was no one there. Everything was in the state in which it had been left.

"Have we been deceived by an illusion?" murmured Cyrus Harding.

No! that was not possible! The telegram had clearly said—

"Come to the corral immediately."

They approached the table specially devoted to the use of the wire. Everything was in order—the pile and the box containing it, as well as all the apparatus.

"Who came here the last time?" asked the engineer.

"I did, captain," answered Ayrton.

"And that was—"

"Four days ago."

"Ah! a note!" cried Herbert, pointing to a paper lying on the table.

On this paper were written these words in English:—

"Follow the new wire."

"Forward!" cried Harding, who understood that the despatch had not been sent from the corral, but from the mysterious retreat, communicating directly with Granite House by means of a supplementary wire joined to the old one.

Neb took the lighted lantern, and all left the corral. The storm then burst forth with tremendous violence. The interval between each lightning-flash and each thunder-clap diminished rapidly. The summit of the volcano, with its plume of vapour, could be seen by occasional flashes.

There was no telegraphic communication in any part of the corral between the house and the palisade; but the engineer, running straight to the first post, saw by the light of a flash a new wire hanging from the isolater to the ground.

"There it is!" said he.

This wire lay along the ground, and was surrounded with an isolating substance like a submarine cable, so as to assure the free transmission of the current. It appeared to pass through the wood and the southern spurs of the mountain, and consequently it ran towards the west.

"Follow it!" said Cyrus Harding.

And the settlers immediately pressed forward, guided by the wire.

The thunder continued to roar with such violence that not a word could be heard. However, there was no occasion for speaking, but to get forward as fast as possible.

Cyrus Harding and his companions then climbed the spur rising between the corral valley and that of Falls River, which they crossed at its narrowest part. The wire, sometimes stretched over the lower branches of the trees, sometimes lying on the ground, guided them surely. The engineer had supposed that the wire would perhaps stop at the bottom of the valley, and that the stranger's retreat would be there.

Nothing of the sort. They were obliged to ascend the south-western spur, and re-descend on that arid plateau terminated by the strangely-wild basalt cliff. From time to time one of the colonists stooped down and felt for the wire with his hands; but there was now no doubt that the wire was running directly towards the sea. There, to a certainty, in the depths of those rocks, was the dwelling so long sought for in vain.

The sky was literally on fire. Flash succeeded flash. Several struck the summit of the volcano in the midst of the thick smoke. It appeared there as if the mountain was vomiting flame. At a few minutes to eleven the colonists arrived on the high cliff overlooking the ocean to the west. The wind had risen. The surf roared 500 feet below.

Harding calculated that they had gone a mile and a half from the coral.

At this point the wire entered among the rocks, following the steep side of a narrow ravine. The settlers followed it at the risk of occasioning a fall of the slightly-balanced rocks, and being dashed into the sea. The descent was extremely perilous, but they did not think of the danger; they were no longer masters of themselves, and an irresistible attraction drew them towards this mysterious place as the magnet draws iron.

Thus they almost unconsciously descended this ravine, which even in broad daylight would have been considered impracticable.

The stones rolled and sparkled like fiery balls when they crossed through the gleams of light. Harding was first—Ayrton last. On they went, step by step. Now they slid over the slippery rock; then they struggled to their feet and scrambled on.

At last the wire touched the rocks on the beach. The colonists had reached the bottom of the basalt cliff.

There appeared a narrow ridge, running horizontally and parallel with the sea. The settlers followed the wire along it. They had not gone a hundred paces when the ridge by a moderate incline sloped down to the level of the sea.

The engineer seized the wire and found that it disappeared beneath the waves.

His companions were stupefied.

A cry of disappointment, almost a cry of despair, escaped them! Must they then plunge beneath the water and seek there for some submarine cavern? In their excited state they would not have hesitated to do it.

The engineer stopped them.

He led his companions to a hollow in the rocks, and there—

"We must wait," said he. "The tide is high. At low-water the way will be open."

"But what can make you think—" asked Pencroft.

"He would not have called us if the means had been wanting to enable us to reach him!"

Cyrus Harding spoke in a tone of such thorough conviction that no objection was raised. His remark, besides, was logical. It was quite possible that an opening, practicable at low-water, though hidden now by the high tide, opened at the foot of the cliff.

There was some time to wait. The colonists remained silently crouching in a deep hollow. Rain now began to fall in torrents. The thunder was re-echoed among the rocks with a grand sonorousness.

The colonists' emotion was great. A thousand strange and extraordinary ideas crossed their brains, and they expected some grand and superhuman apparition, which alone could come up to the notion they had formed of the mysterious genius of the island.

At midnight, Harding, carrying the lantern, descended to the beach to reconnoitre.

The engineer was not mistaken. The beginning of an immense excavation could be seen under the water. There the wire, bending at a right angle, entered the yawning gulf.

Cyrus Harding returned to his companions, and said simply—

"In an hour the opening will be practicable."

"It is there, then?" said Pencroft.

"Did you doubt it?" returned Harding.

"But this cavern must be filled with water to a certain height," observed Herbert.

"Either the cavern will be completely dry," replied Harding, "and in that case we can traverse it on foot, or it will not be dry, and some means of transport will be put at our disposal."

An hour passed. All climbed down through the rain to the level of the sea. There was now eight feet of the opening above the water. It was like the arch of a bridge, under which rushed the foaming water.

Leaning forward, the engineer saw a black object floating on the water. He drew it towards him. It was a boat, moored to some interior projection of the cave. This boat was iron-plated. Two oars lay at the bottom.

"Jump in!" said Harding.

In a moment the settlers were in the boat. Neb and Ayrton took the oars, Pencroft the rudder. Cyrus Harding in the bows, with the lantern, lighted the way.

The elliptical roof, under which the boat at first passed, suddenly rose; but the darkness was too deep, and the light of the lantern too slight, for either the extent, length, height, or depth of the cave to be ascertained. Solemn silence reigned in this basaltic cavern. Not a sound could penetrate into it, even the thunder peals could not pierce its thick sides.

Such immense caves exist in various parts of the world, natural crypts dating from the geological epoch of the globe. Some are filled by the sea; others contain entire lakes in their sides. Such is Fingal's Cave, in the island of Staffa, one of the Hebrides; such are the caves of Morgat, in the bay of Douarucuez, in Brittany, the caves of Bonifacier, in Corsica, those of Lyse-Fjord, in Norway; such are the immense Mammoth caverns in Kentucky, 500 feet in height, and more than twenty miles in length! In many parts of the globe, nature has excavated these caverns, and preserved them for the admiration of man.

Did the cavern which the settlers were now exploring extend to the centre of the island? For a quarter of an hour the boat had been advancing, making *detours*, indicated to Pencroft by the engineer in short sentences, when all at once—

"More to the right!" he commanded. The boat, altering its course, came up alongside the right wall. The engineer wished to see if the wire still ran along the side. The wire was there fastened to the rock. "Forward!" said Harding.

And the two oars, plunging into the dark waters, urged the boat onwards.

On they went for another quarter of an hour, and a distance of half-a-mile must have been cleared from the mouth of the cave, when Harding's voice was again heard. "Stop!" said he.

The boat stopped, and the colonists perceived a bright light illuminating the vast cavern, so deeply excavated in the bowels of the island, of which nothing had ever led them to suspect the existence.

At a height of a hundred feet rose the vaulted roof, supported on basalt shafts. Irregular arches, strange mouldings, appeared on the columns erected by nature in thousands from the first epochs of the formation of the globe. The basalt pillars, fitted one into the other, measured from forty to fifty feet in height, and the water, calm in spite of the tumult outside, washing their base. The brilliant focus of light, pointed out by the engineer, touched every point of rock, and flooded the walls with light. By reflection the water reproduced the brilliant sparkles, so that the boat appeared to be floating between two glittering zones.

They could not be mistaken in the nature of the irradiation thrown from the centre light, whose clear rays broke all the angles, all the projections of the cavern. This light proceeded from an electric source, and its white colour betrayed its origin. It was the sun of this cave, and it filled it entirely.

At a sign from Cyrus Harding the oars again plunged into the water, causing a regular shower of gems, and the boat was urged forward towards the light, which was now not more than half a cable's length distant.

At this place the breadth of the sheet of water measured nearly 350 feet, and beyond the dazzling centre could be seen an enormous basaltic wall, blocking up any issue on that side. The cavern widened here considerably, the sea forming a little lake. But the roof, the side walls, the end cliff, all the prisms, all the peaks, were flooded with the electric fluid, so that the brilliancy belonged to them, and as if the light issued from them.

In the centre of the lake a long cigar-shaped object floated on the surface of the water, silent, motionless. The brilliancy which issued from it escaped from its sides as from two kilns heated to a white heat. This apparatus, similar in shape to an enormous whale, was about 250 feet long, and rose about ten or twelve above the water.

The boat slowly approached it. Cyrus Harding stood up in the bows. He gazed, a prey to violent excitement. Then, all at once, seizing the reporter's arm—

"It is he! It can only be he!" he cried, "he!—"

Then, falling back on the seat, he murmured a name which Gideon Spilett alone could hear.

The reporter evidently knew this name, for it had a wonderful effect upon him, and he answered in a hoarse voice—

"He! an outlawed man!"

"He!" said Harding.

At the engineer's command the boat approached this singular floating apparatus. The boat touched the left side, from which escaped a ray of light through a thick glass.

Harding and his companions mounted on the platform. An open hatchway was there. All darted down the opening.

At the bottom of the ladder was a deck, lighted by electricity. At the end of this deck was a door, which Harding opened.

A richly-ornamented room, quickly traversed by the colonists, was joined to a library, over which a luminous ceiling shed a flood of light.

At the end of the library a large door, also shut, was opened by the engineer.

An immense saloon—a sort of museum, in which were heaped up, with all the treasures of the mineral world, works of art, marvels of industry—appeared before the eyes of the colonists, who almost thought themselves suddenly transported into a land of enchantment.

Stretched on a rich sofa they saw a man, who did not appear to notice their presence.

Then Harding raised his voice, and to the extreme surprise of his companions, he uttered these words—

"Captain Nemo, you asked for us! We are here."

XVI

Captain Nemo—His first Words—The History of
the Recluse—His Adventures—His Sentiments—
His Comrades—Submarine Life—Alone—The last
Refuge of the Nautilus in Lincoln Island—
The Mysterious Genius of the Island.

At these words the reclining figure rose, and the electric light fell upon his countenance; a magnificent head, the forehead high, the glance commanding, beard white, hair abundant and falling over the shoulders.

His hand rested upon the cushion of the divan from which he had just risen. He appeared perfectly calm. It was evident that his strength had been gradually undermined by illness, but his voice seemed yet powerful, as he said in English, and in a tone which evinced extreme surprise—

"Sir, I have no name."

"Nevertheless, I know you!" replied Cyrus Harding.

Captain Nemo fixed his penetrating gaze upon the engineer as though he were about to annihilate him.

Then, falling back amid the pillows of the divan—

"After all, what matters now?" he murmured; "I am dying!"

Cyrus Harding drew near the captain, and Gideon Spilett took his hand—it was of a feverish heat. Ayrton, Pencroft, Herbert, and Neb, stood respectfully apart in an angle of the magnificent saloon, whose atmosphere was saturated with the electric fluid.

Meanwhile Captain Nemo withdrew his hand, and motioned the engineer and the reporter to be seated.

All regarded him with profound emotion. Before them they beheld that being whom they had styled the "genius of the island," the powerful protector whose intervention, in so many circumstances, had been so efficacious, the benefactor to whom they owed such a debt of gratitude! Their eyes beheld a man only, and a man at the point of death, where Pencroft and Neb had expected to find an almost supernatural being!

But how happened it that Cyrus Harding had recognised Captain Nemo? Why had the latter so suddenly risen on hearing this name uttered, a name which he had believed known to none?

The captain had resumed his position on the divan, and leaning on his arm, he regarded the engineer, seated near him.

"You know the name I formerly bore, sir?" he asked.

"I do," answered Cyrus Harding, "and also that of this wonderful submarine vessel—"

"The *Nautilus*?" said the captain, with a faint smile.

"The *Nautilus*!"

"But do you—do you know who I am?"

"I do."

"It is nevertheless many years since I have held any communication with the inhabited world; three long years have I passed in the depths of the sea, the only place where I have found liberty! Who then can have betrayed my secret?"

"A man who was bound to you by no tie, Captain Nemo, and who, consequently, cannot be accused of treachery."

"The Frenchman who was cast on board my vessel by chance sixteen years since?"

"The same."

"He and his two companions did not then perish in the Maelstrom, in the midst of which the *Nautilus* was struggling."

"They escaped, and a book has appeared under the title of *Twenty Thousand Leagues under the Sea*, which contains your history."

"The history of a few months only of my life!" interrupted the captain impetuously.

"It is true," answered Cyrus Harding, "but a few months of that strange life have sufficed to make you known—"

"As a great criminal, doubtless!" said Captain Nemo, a haughty smile curling his lips. "Yes, a rebel, perhaps an outlaw against humanity!"

The engineer was silent.

"Well, sir?"

"It is not for me to judge you, Captain Nemo," answered Cyrus Harding, "at any rate as regards your past life. I am, with the rest of the world, ignorant of the motives which induced you to adopt this strange mode of existence, and I cannot judge of effects without knowing their causes; but what I *do* know is, that a beneficent hand has constantly protected us since our arrival on Lincoln Island, that we all owe our lives to a good, generous, and powerful being, and that this being so powerful, good and generous, Captain Nemo, is yourself!"

"It is I," answered the captain simply.

The engineer and reporter rose. Their companions had drawn near, and the gratitude with which their hearts were charged was about to express itself in their gestures and words.

Captain Nemo stopped them by a sign, and in a voice which betrayed more emotion than he doubtless intended to show.

"Wait till you have heard all," he said.

And the captain, in a few concise sentences, ran over the events of his life.

His narrative was short, yet he was obliged to summon up his whole remaining energy to arrive at the end. He was evidently contending against extreme weakness. Several times Cyrus Harding entreated him to repose for a while, but he shook his head as a man to whom the morrow may never come, and when the reporter offered his assistance—

"It is useless," he said; "my hours are numbered."

Captain Nemo was an Indian, the Prince Dakkar, son of a rajah of the then independent territory of Bundelkund. His father sent him, when ten years of age, to Europe, in order that he might receive an education in all respects complete, and in the hopes that by his talents and knowledge he might one day take a leading part in raising his long degraded and heathen country to a level with the nations of Europe.

From the age of ten years to that of thirty Prince Dakkar, endowed by Nature with her richest gifts of intellect, accumulated knowledge of every kind, and in science, literature, and art his researches were extensive and profound.

He travelled over the whole of Europe. His rank and fortune caused him to be everywhere sought after; but the pleasures of the world had for him no attractions. Though young and possessed of every personal advantage, he was ever grave—sombre even—devoured by an unquenchable thirst for knowledge, and cherishing in the recesses of his heart the hope that he might become a great and powerful ruler of a free and enlightened people.

Still, for long the love of science triumphed over all other feelings. He became an artist deeply impressed by the marvels of art, a philosopher to whom no one of the higher sciences was unknown, a statesman versed in the policy of European courts. To the eyes of those who observed him superficially he might have passed for one of those cosmopolitans, curious of knowledge, but disdaining action; one of those opulent travellers, haughty and cynical, who move incessantly from place to place, and are of no country.

This artist, this philosopher, this man was, however, still cherishing the hope instilled into him from his earliest days.

Prince Dakkar returned to Bundelkund in the year 1849. He married a noble Indian lady, who was imbued with an ambition not less ardent than that by which he was inspired. Two children were born to them, whom they tenderly loved. But domestic happiness did not prevent him from seeking to carry out the object at which he aimed. He waited an opportunity. At length, as he vainly fancied, it presented itself.

Instigated by princes equally ambitious and less sagacious and more unscrupulous than he was, the people of India were persuaded that they might successfully rise against their English rulers, who had brought them out of a state of anarchy and constant warfare and misery, and had established peace and prosperity in their country. Their ignorance and gross superstition made them the facile tools of their designing chiefs.

In 1857 the great sepoy revolt broke out. Prince Dakkar, under the belief that he should thereby have the opportunity of attaining the object of his long-cherished ambition, was easily drawn into it. He forthwith devoted his talents and wealth to the service of this cause. He aided it in person; he fought in the front ranks; he risked his life equally with the humblest of the wretched and misguided fanatics; he was ten times wounded in twenty engagements, seeking death but finding it not, when at length the sanguinary rebels were utterly defeated, and the atrocious mutiny was brought to an end.

Never before had the British power in India been exposed to such danger, and if, as they had hoped, the sepoys had received assistance from without, the influence and supremacy in Asia of the United Kingdom would have been a thing of the past.

The name of Prince Dakkar was at that time well-known. He had fought openly and without concealment. A price was set upon his head, but he managed to escape from his pursuers.

Civilisation never recedes; the law of necessity ever forces it onwards. The sepoys were vanquished, and the land of the rajahs of old fell again under the rule of England.

Prince Dakkar, unable to find that death he courted, returned to the mountain fastnesses of Bundelkund. There, alone in the world, overcome by disappointment at the destruction of all his vain hopes, a prey to profound disgust for all human beings, filled with hatred of the civilised world, he realised the wreck of his fortune, assembled some score of his most faithful companions, and one day disappeared, leaving no trace behind.

Where, then, did he seek that liberty denied him upon the inhabited earth? Under the waves, in the depths of the ocean, where none could follow.

The warrior became the man of science. Upon a deserted island of the Pacific he established his dockyard, and there a submarine vessel was constructed from his designs. By methods which will at some future day be revealed he had rendered subservient the illimitable forces of electricity, which, extracted from inexhaustible sources, was employed for all the requirements of his floating equipage, as a moving, lighting, and heating agent. The sea, with its countless treasures, its myriads of fish, its numberless wrecks, its enormous mammalia, and not only all that nature supplied, but also all that man had lost in its depths, sufficed for every want of the prince and his crew—and thus was his most ardent desire accomplished, never again to hold communication with the earth. He named his submarine vessel the *Nautilus*, called himself simply Captain Nemo, and disappeared beneath the seas.

During many years this strange being visited every ocean, from pole to pole. Outcast of the inhabited earth in these unknown worlds he gathered incalculable treasures. The millions lost in the Bay of Vigo, in 1702, by the galleons of Spain, furnished him with a mine of inexhaustible riches which he devoted always, anonymously, in favour of those nations who fought for the independence of their country.

For long, however, he had held no communication with his fellow-creatures, when, during the night of the 6th of November, 1866, three men were cast on board his vessel. They were a French professor, his servant, and a Canadian fisherman. These three men had been hurled overboard by a collision which had taken place between the *Nautilus* and the United States frigate *Abraham Lincoln*, which had chased her.

Captain Nemo learnt from this professor that the *Nautilus*, taken now for a gigantic mammal of the whale species, now for a submarine vessel carrying a crew of pirates, was sought for in every sea.

He might have returned these three men to the ocean, from whence chance had brought them in contact with his mysterious existence. Instead of doing this he kept them prisoners, and during seven months they were enabled to behold all the wonders of a voyage of twenty thousand leagues under the sea.

One day, the 22nd of June, 1867, these three men, who knew nothing of the past history of Captain Nemo, succeeded in escaping in one of the *Nautilus's* boats. But as at this time the *Nautilus* was drawn into the vortex of the Maelstrom, off the coast of Norway, the captain naturally believed that the fugitives, engulfed in that frightful whirlpool, found their death at the bottom of the abyss. He was ignorant that the Frenchman and his two companions had been miraculously cast on shore, that the fishermen of the Loffoden Islands had rendered them assistance, and that the professor, on his return to France, had published that work in which seven months of the strange and eventful navigation of the *Nautilus* were narrated and exposed to the curiosity of the public.

For a long time after this, Captain Nemo continued to live thus, traversing every sea. But one by one his companions died, and found their last resting-place in their cemetery of coral, in the bed of the Pacific. At last Captain Nemo remained the solitary survivor of all those who had taken refuge with him in the depths of the ocean.

He was now sixty years of age. Although alone, he succeeded in navigating the *Nautilus* towards one of those submarine caverns which had sometimes served him as a harbour.

One of these ports was hollowed beneath Lincoln Island, and at this moment furnished an asylum to the *Nautilus*.

The captain had now remained there six years, navigating the ocean no longer, but awaiting death, and that moment when he should rejoin his former companions, when by chance he observed the descent of the balloon which carried the prisoners of the Confederates. Clad in his diving-dress he was walking beneath the water at a few cables' length from the shore of the island, when the engineer had been thrown into the sea. Moved by a feeling of compassion the captain saved Cyrus Harding.

His first impulse was to fly from the vicinity of the five castaways; but his harbour of refuge was closed, for in consequence of an elevation of the basalt, produced by the influence of volcanic action, he could no longer pass through the entrance of the vault. Though there was sufficient depth of water to allow a light craft to pass the bar, there was not enough for the *Nautilus*, whose draught of water was considerable.

Captain Nemo was compelled, therefore, to remain. He observed these men thrown without resources upon a desert island, but had no wish to be himself discovered by them. By degrees he became interested in their efforts when he saw them honest, energetic, and bound to each other by the ties of friendship. As if despite his wishes, he penetrated all the secrets of their existence. By means of the diving-dress he could easily reach the well in the interior of Granite House, and climbing by the projections of rock to its upper orifice he heard the colonists as they recounted the past, and studied the present and future. He learnt from them the tremendous conflict of America with America itself, for the abolition of slavery. Yes, these men were worthy to reconcile Captain Nemo with that humanity which they represented so nobly in the island.

Captain Nemo had saved Cyrus Harding. It was he also who had brought back the dog to the Chimneys, who rescued Top from the waters of the lake, who caused to fall at Flotsam Point the case containing so many things useful to the colonists, who conveyed the canoe back into the stream of the Mercy, who cast the cord from the top of Granite House at the time of the attack by the baboons, who made known the presence of Ayrton upon Tabor Island, by means of the document enclosed in the bottle, who caused the explosion of the brig by the shock of a torpedo placed at the bottom of the canal, who saved Herbert from a certain death by bringing the sulphate of quinine; and finally, it was he who had killed the convicts with the electric balls, of which he possessed the secret, and which he employed in the chase of submarine creatures. Thus were explained so many apparently supernatural occurrences, and which all proved the generosity and power of the captain.

Nevertheless, this noble misanthrope longed to benefit his *proteges* still further. There yet remained much useful advice to give them, and, his heart being softened by the approach of death, he invited, as we are aware, the colonists of Granite House to visit the *Nautilus*, by means of a wire which connected it with the corral. Possibly he would not have done this had he been aware that Cyrus Harding was sufficiently acquainted with his history to address him by the name of Nemo.

The captain concluded the narrative of his life. Cyrus Harding then spoke; he recalled all the incidents which had exercised so beneficent an influence upon the colony, and in the names of his companions and himself thanked the generous being to whom they owed so much.

But Captain Nemo paid little attention; his mind appeared to be absorbed by one idea, and without taking the proffered hand of the engineer—

"Now, sir," said he, "now that you know my history, your judgment!"

In saying this, the captain evidently alluded to an important incident witnessed by the three strangers thrown on board his vessel, and which the French professor had related in his work, causing a profound and terrible sensation. Some days previous to the flight of the professor and his two companions, the *Nautilus*, being chased by a frigate in the north of the Atlantic, had hurled herself as a ram upon this frigate, and sunk her without mercy.

Cyrus Harding understood the captain's allusion, and was silent.

"It was an enemy's frigate," exclaimed Captain Nemo, transformed for an instant into the Prince Dakkar, "an enemy's frigate! It was she who attacked me—I was in a narrow and shallow bay—the frigate barred my way—and I sank her!"

A few moments of silence ensued; then the captain demanded—

"What think you of my life, gentlemen?"

Cyrus Harding extended his hand to the ci-devant prince and replied gravely, "Sir, your error was in supposing that the past can be resuscitated, and in contending against inevitable progress. It is one of those errors which some admire, others blame; which God alone can judge. He who is mistaken in an action which he sincerely believes to be right may be an enemy, but retains our esteem. Your error is one that we may admire, and your name has nothing to fear from the judgment of history, which does not condemn heroic folly, but its results."

The old man's breast swelled with emotion, and raising his hand to heaven—

"Was I wrong, or in the right?" he murmured.

Cyrus Harding replied, "All great actions return to God, from whom they are derived. Captain Nemo, we, whom you have succoured, shall ever mourn your loss."

Herbert, who had drawn near the captain, fell on his knees and kissed his hand.

A tear glistened in the eyes of the dying man. "My child," he said, "may God bless you!"

XVII

Last Moments of Captain Nemo—Wishes of the dying
Man—A Parting Gift to his Friends of a Day—Captain
Nemo's Coffin—Advice to the Colonists—The supreme
Moment—At the Bottom of the Sea.

Day had returned. No ray of light penetrated into the profundity
of the cavern. It being high-water, the entrance was closed by
the sea. But the artificial light, which escaped in long streams from the
skylights of the *Nautilus*, was as vivid as before, and the sheet of water
shone around the floating vessel.

An extreme exhaustion now overcame Captain Nemo, who had
fallen back upon the divan. It was useless to contemplate removing
him to Granite House, for he had expressed his wish to remain in
the midst of those marvels of the *Nautilus* which millions could not
have purchased, and to await there for that death which was swiftly
approaching.

During a long interval of prostration, which rendered him almost
unconscious, Cyrus Harding and Gideon Spilett attentively observed
the condition of the dying man. It was apparent that his strength was
gradually diminishing. That frame, once so robust, was now but the
fragile tenement of a departing soul. All of life was concentrated in the
heart and head.

The engineer and reporter consulted in whispers. Was it possible
to render any aid to the dying man? Might his life, if not saved, be
prolonged for some days? He himself had said that no remedy could
avail, and he awaited with tranquillity that death which had for him
no terrors.

"We can do nothing," said Gideon Spilett.

"But of what is he dying?" asked Pencroft.

"Life is simply fading out," replied the reporter.

"Nevertheless," said the sailor, "if we moved him into the open air,
and the light of the sun, he might perhaps recover."

"No, Pencroft," answered the engineer, "it is useless to attempt it.
Besides, Captain Nemo would never consent to leave his vessel. He has
lived for a dozen years on board the *Nautilus*, and on board the *Nautilus*
he desires to die."

Without doubt Captain Nemo heard Cyrus Harding's reply, for he raised himself slightly, and in a voice more feeble, but always intelligible—

"You are right, sir," he said. "I shall die here—it is my wish; and therefore I have a request to make of you."

Cyrus Harding and his companions had drawn near the divan, and now arranged the cushions in such a manner as to better support the dying man.

They saw his eyes wander over all the marvels of this saloon, lighted by the electric rays which fell from the arabesques of the luminous ceiling. He surveyed, one after the other, the pictures hanging from the splendid tapestries of the partitions, the *chef-d'oeuvres* of the Italian, Flemish, French, and Spanish masters; the statues of marble and bronze on their pedestals; the magnificent organ, leaning against the after-partition; the aquarium, in which bloomed the most wonderful productions of the sea—marine plants, zoophytes, chaplets of pearls of inestimable value; and, finally, his eyes rested on this device, inscribed over the pediment of the museum—the motto of the *Nautilus*—

"*Mobilis in mobile.*"

His glance seemed to rest fondly for the last time on these masterpieces of art and of nature, to which he had limited his horizon during a sojourn of so many years in the abysses of the seas.

Cyrus Harding respected the captain's silence, and waited till he should speak.

After some minutes, during which, doubtless, he passed in review his whole life, Captain Nemo turned to the colonists and said—

"You consider yourselves, gentlemen, under some obligations to me?"

"Captain, believe us that we would give our lives to prolong yours."

"Promise, then," continued Captain Nemo, "to carry out my last wishes, and I shall be repaid for all I have done for you."

"We promise," said Cyrus Harding.

And by this promise he bound both himself and his companions.

"Gentlemen," resumed the captain, "to-morrow I shall be dead."

Herbert was about to utter an exclamation, but a sign from the captain arrested him.

"To-morrow I shall die, and I desire no other tomb than the *Nautilus*. It is my grave! All my friends repose in the depths of the ocean; their resting-place shall be mine."

These words were received with profound silence.

"Pay attention to my wishes," he continued. "The *Nautilus* is imprisoned in this grotto, the entrance of which is blocked up; but, although egress is impossible, the vessel may at least sink in the abyss, and there bury my remains."

The colonists listened reverently to the words of the dying man.

"To-morrow, after my death, Mr. Harding," continued the captain, "yourself and companions will leave the *Nautilus*, for all the treasures it contains must perish with me. One token alone will remain with you of Prince Dakkar, with whose history you are now acquainted. That coffer yonder contains diamonds of the value of many millions, most of them mementoes of the time when, husband and father, I thought happiness possible for me, and a collection of pearls gathered by my friends and myself in the depths of the ocean. Of this treasure, at a future day, you may make good use. In the hands of such men as yourself and your comrades, Captain Harding, money will never be a source of danger. From on high I shall still participate in your enterprises, and I fear not but that they will prosper."

After a few moments' repose, necessitated by his extreme weakness, Captain Nemo continued—

"To-morrow you will take the coffer, you will leave the saloon, of which you will close the door; then you will ascend onto the deck of the *Nautilus*, and you will lower the main-hatch so as entirely to close the vessel."

"It shall be done, captain," answered Cyrus Harding.

"Good. You will then embark in the canoe which brought you hither; but, before leaving the *Nautilus*, go to the stern and there open two large stop-cocks which you will find upon the water-line. The water will penetrate into the reservoirs, and the *Nautilus* will gradually sink beneath the water to repose at the bottom of the abyss."

And, comprehending a gesture of Cyrus Harding, the captain added—

"Fear nothing! You will but bury a corpse!"

Neither Cyrus Harding nor his companions ventured to offer any observation to Captain Nemo. He had expressed his last wishes, and they had nothing to do but to conform to them.

"I have your promise, gentlemen?" added Captain Nemo.

"You have, captain," replied the engineer.

The captain thanked the colonists by a sign, and requested them to leave him for some hours. Gideon Spilett wished to remain near him, in the event of a crisis coming on, but the dying man refused, saying, "I shall live until to-morrow, sir."

All left the saloon, passed through the library and the dining-room, and arrived forward, in the machine-room, where the electrical apparatus was established, which supplied not only heat and light but the mechanical power of the *Nautilus*.

The *Nautilus* was a masterpiece, containing masterpieces within itself, and the engineer was struck with astonishment.

The colonists mounted the platform, which rose seven or eight feet above the water. There they beheld a thick glass lenticular covering, which protected a kind of large eye, from which flashed forth light. Behind this eye was apparently a cabin containing the wheels of the rudder, and in which was stationed the helmsman, when he navigated the *Nautilus* over the bed of the ocean, which the electric rays would evidently light up to a considerable distance.

Cyrus Harding and his companions remained for a time silent, for they were vividly impressed by what they had just seen and heard, and their hearts were deeply touched by the thought that he whose arm had so often aided them, the protector whom they had known but a few hours, was at the point of death.

Whatever might be the judgment pronounced by posterity upon the events of this, so to speak, extra-human existence, the character of Prince Dakkar would ever remain as one of those whose memory time can never efface.

"What a man!" said Pencroft. "Is it possible that he can have lived at the bottom of the sea? And it seems to me that perhaps he has not found peace there any more than elsewhere."

"The *Nautilus*," observed Ayrton, "might have enabled us to leave Lincoln Island and reach some inhabited country."

"Good Heavens!" exclaimed Pencroft, "I for one would never risk myself in such a craft. To sail on the seas, good; but under the seas, never!"

"I believe, Pencroft," answered the reporter, "that the navigation of a submarine vessel such as the *Nautilus* ought to be very easy, and that we should soon become accustomed to it. There would be no storms, no lee-shore to fear. At some feet beneath the surface the waters of the ocean are as calm as those of a lake."

"That may be," replied the sailor, "but I prefer a gale of wind on board a well-found craft. A vessel is built to sail on the sea, and not beneath it."

"My friends," said the engineer, "it is useless, at any rate as regards the *Nautilus*, to discuss the question of submarine vessels. The *Nautilus* is not ours, and we have not the right to dispose of it. Moreover, we could in no case avail ourselves of it. Independently of the fact that it would be impossible to get it out of this cavern, whose entrance is now closed by the uprising of the basaltic rocks, Captain Nemo's wish is that it shall be buried with him. His wish is our law, and we will fulfil it."

After a somewhat prolonged conversation, Cyrus Harding and his companions again descended to the interior of the *Nautilus*. There they took some refreshment and returned to the saloon.

Captain Nemo had somewhat rallied from the prostration which had overcome him, and his eyes shone with their wonted fire. A faint smile even curled his lips.

The colonists drew around him.

"Gentlemen," said the captain, "you are brave and honest men. You have devoted yourselves to the common weal. Often have I observed your conduct. I have esteemed you—I esteem you still! Your hand, Mr. Harding!"

Cyrus Harding gave his hand to the captain, who clasped it affectionately.

"It is well!" he murmured.

He resumed—

"But enough of myself. I have to speak concerning yourselves, and this Lincoln Island, upon which you have taken refuge. You desire to leave it?"

"To return, captain!" answered Pencroft quickly.

"To return, Pencroft?" said the captain, with a smile. "I know, it is true, your love for this island. You have helped to make it what it now is, and it seems to you a paradise!"

"Our project, captain," interposed Cyrus Harding, "is to annex it to the United States, and to establish for our shipping a port so fortunately situated in this part of the Pacific."

"Your thoughts are with your country, gentlemen," continued the captain; "your toils are for her prosperity and glory. You are right. One's native land!—there should one live! there die! And I! I die far from all I loved!"

"You have some last wish to transmit," said the engineer with emotion, "some souvenir to send to those friends you have left in the mountains of India?"

"No, Captain Harding; no friends remain to me! I am the last of my race, and to all whom I have known I have long been as are the dead.— But to return to yourselves. Solitude, isolation, are painful things, and beyond human endurance. I die of having thought it possible to live alone! You should, therefore, dare all in the attempt to leave Lincoln Island, and see once more the land of your birth. I am aware that those wretches have destroyed the vessel you had built."

"We propose to construct a vessel," said Gideon Spilett, "sufficiently large to convey us to the nearest land; but if we should succeed, sooner or later we shall return to Lincoln Island. We are attached to it by too many recollections ever to forget it."

"It is here that we have known Captain Nemo," said Cyrus Harding.

"It is here only that we can make our home!" added Herbert.

"And here shall I sleep the sleep of eternity, if—" replied the captain.

He paused for a moment, and, instead of completing the sentence, said simply—

"Mr. Harding, I wish to speak with you—alone!"

The engineer's companions, respecting the wish of the dying man, retired.

Cyrus Harding remained but a few minutes alone with Captain Nemo, and soon recalled his companions; but he said nothing to them of the private matters which the dying man had confided to him.

Gideon Spilett now watched the captain with extreme care. It was evident that he was no longer sustained by his moral energy, which had lost the power of reaction against his physical weakness.

The day closed without change. The colonists did not quit the *Nautilus* for a moment. Night arrived, although it was impossible to distinguish it from day in the cavern.

Captain Nemo suffered no pain, but he was visibly sinking. His noble features, paled by the approach of death, were perfectly calm. Inaudible words escaped at intervals from his lips, bearing upon various incidents of his chequered career. Life was evidently ebbing slowly, and his extremities were already cold.

Once or twice more he spoke to the colonists who stood around him, and smiled on them with that last smile which continues after death.

At length, shortly after midnight, Captain Nemo by a supreme effort succeeded in folding his arms across his breast, as if wishing in that attitude to compose himself for death.

By one o'clock his glance alone showed signs of life. A dying light gleamed in those eyes once so brilliant. Then, murmuring the words, "God and my country!" he quietly expired.

Cyrus Harding, bending low, closed the eyes of him who had once been the Prince Dakkar, and was now not even Captain Nemo.

Herbert and Pencroft sobbed aloud. Tears fell from Ayrton's eyes. Neb was on his knees by the reporter's side, motionless as a statue.

Then Cyrus Harding, extending his hand over the forehead of the dead, said solemnly—

"May his soul be with God! Let us pray!"

Some hours later the colonists fulfilled the promise made to the captain by carrying out his dying wishes.

Cyrus Harding and his companions quitted the *Nautilus*, taking with them the only memento left them by their benefactor, that coffer which contained wealth amounting to millions.

The marvellous saloon, still flooded with light, had been carefully closed. The iron door leading on deck was then securely fastened in such a manner as to prevent even a drop of water from penetrating to the interior of the *Nautilus*.

The colonists then descended into the canoe, which was moored to the side of the submarine vessel.

The canoe was now brought round to the stern. There, at the water-line, were two large stop-cocks, communicating with the reservoirs employed in the submersion of the vessel.

The stop-cocks were opened, the reservoirs filled, and the *Nautilus*, slowly sinking, disappeared beneath the surface of the lake.

But the colonists were yet able to follow its descent through the waves. The powerful light it gave forth lighted up the translucent water, while the cavern became gradually obscure. At length this vast effusion of electric light faded away, and soon after the *Nautilus*, now the tomb of Captain Nemo, reposed in its ocean bed.

XVIII

REFLECTIONS OF THE COLONISTS—THEIR LABOURS OF
RECONSTRUCTION RESUMED—THE 1ST OF JANUARY 1869—
A CLOUD OVER THE SUMMIT OF THE VOLCANO—FIRST WARNINGS
OF AN ERUPTION—AYRTON AND CYRUS HARDING AT THE
CORRAL—EXPLORATION OF THE DAKKAR GROTTO—WHAT
CAPTAIN NEMO HAD CONFIDED TO THE ENGINEER.

At break of day the colonists regained in silence the entrance of
the cavern, to which they gave the name of "Dakkar Grotto," in
memory of Captain Nemo. It was now low-water, and they passed
without difficulty under the arcade, washed on the right by the sea.

The canoe was left here, carefully protected from the waves. As an
excess of precaution, Pencroft, Neb, and Ayrton drew it up on a little
beach which bordered one of the sides of the grotto, in a spot where it
could run no risk of harm.

The storm had ceased during the night. The last low mutterings of
the thunder died away in the west. Rain fell no longer, but the sky was
yet obscured by clouds. On the whole, this month of October, the first
of the southern spring, was not ushered in by satisfactory tokens, and
the wind had a tendency to shift from one point of the compass to
another, which rendered it impossible to count upon settled weather.

Cyrus Harding and his companions, on leaving Dakkar Grotto, had
taken the road to the corral. On their way Neb and Herbert were careful
to preserve the wire which had been laid down by the captain between
the corral and the grotto, and which might at a future time be of service.

The colonists spoke but little on the road. The various incidents
of the night of the 15th October had left a profound impression on
their minds. The unknown being whose influence had so effectually
protected them, the man whom their imagination had endowed with
supernatural powers, Captain Nemo, was no more. His *Nautilus* and
he were buried in the depths of the abyss. To each one of them their
existence seemed even more isolated than before. They had been
accustomed to count upon the intervention of that power which existed
no longer, and Gideon Spilett, and even Cyrus Harding, could not
escape this impression. Thus they maintained a profound silence during
their journey to the corral.

Towards nine in the morning the colonists arrived at Granite House.

It had been agreed that the construction of the vessel should be actively pushed forward, and Cyrus Harding more than ever devoted his time and labour to this object. It was impossible to divine what future lay before them. Evidently the advantage to the colonists would be great of having at their disposal a substantial vessel, capable of keeping the sea even in heavy weather, and large enough to attempt, in case of need, a voyage of some duration. Even if, when their vessel should be completed, the colonists should not resolve to leave Lincoln Island as yet, in order to gain either one of the Polynesian archipelagos of the Pacific or the shores of New Zealand, they might at least, sooner or later, proceed to Tabor Island, to leave there the notice relating to Ayrton. This was a precaution rendered indispensable by the possibility of the Scotch yacht reappearing in those seas, and it was of the highest importance that nothing should be neglected on this point.

The works were then resumed. Cyrus Harding, Pencroft, and Ayrton, assisted by Neb, Gideon Spilett, and Herbert, except when unavoidably called off by other necessary occupations, worked without cessation. It was important that the new vessel should be ready in five months—that is to say, by the beginning of March—if they wished to visit Tabor Island before the equinoctial gales rendered the voyage impracticable. Therefore the carpenters lost not a moment. Moreover, it was unnecessary to manufacture rigging, that of the *Speedy* having been saved entire, so that the hull only of the vessel needed to be constructed.

The end of the year 1868 found them occupied by these important labours, to the exclusion of almost all others. At the expiration of two months and a half the ribs had been set up and the first planks adjusted. It was already evident that the plans made by Cyrus Harding were admirable, and that the vessel would behave well at sea.

Pencroft brought to the task a devouring energy, and scrupled not to grumble when one or the other abandoned the carpenter's axe for the gun of the hunter. It was nevertheless necessary to keep up the stores of Granite House, in view of the approaching winter. But this did not satisfy Pencroft. The brave honest sailor was not content when the workmen were not at the dockyard. When this happened he grumbled vigorously, and, by way of venting his feelings, did the work of six men.

The weather was very unfavourable during the whole of the summer season. For some days the heat was overpowering, and the atmosphere, saturated with electricity, was only cleared by violent storms. It was rarely that the distant growling of the thunder could not be heard, like a low but incessant murmur, such as is produced in the equatorial regions of the globe.

The 1st of January, 1869, was signalised by a storm of extreme violence, and the thunder burst several times over the island. Large trees were struck by the electric fluid and shattered, and among others one of those gigantic micocouliers which shaded the poultry-yard at the southern extremity of the lake. Had this meteor any relation to the phenomena going on in the bowels of the earth? Was there any connection between the commotion of the atmosphere and that of the interior of the earth? Cyrus Harding was inclined to think that such was the case, for the development of these storms was attended by the renewal of volcanic symptoms.

It was on the 3rd of January that Herbert, having ascended at daybreak to the plateau of Prospect Heights to harness one of the onagas, perceived an enormous hat-shaped cloud rolling from the summit of the volcano.

Herbert immediately apprised the colonists, who at once joined him in watching the summit of Mount Franklin.

"Ah!" exclaimed Pencroft, "those are not vapours this time! It seems to me that the giant is not content with breathing; he must smoke!"

This figure of speech employed by the sailor exactly expressed the changes going on at the mouth of the volcano. Already for three months had the crater emitted vapours more or less dense, but which were as yet produced only by an internal ebullition of mineral substances. But now the vapours were replaced by a thick smoke, rising in the form of a greyish column, more than three hundred feet in width at its base, and which spread like an immense mushroom to a height of from seven to eight hundred feet above the summit of the mountain.

"The fire is in the chimney," observed Gideon Spilett.

"And we can't put it out!" replied Herbert.

"The volcano ought to be swept," observed Neb, who spoke as if perfectly serious.

"Well said, Neb!" cried Pencroft, with a shout of laughter; "and you'll undertake the job, no doubt?"

Cyrus Harding attentively observed the dense smoke emitted by Mount Franklin, and even listened, as if expecting to hear some distant muttering. Then, turning towards his companions, from whom he had gone somewhat apart, he said—

"The truth is, my friends, we must not conceal from ourselves that an important change is going forward. The volcanic substances are no longer in a state of ebullition, they have caught fire, and we are undoubtedly menaced by an approaching eruption."

"Well, captain," said Pencroft, "we shall witness the eruption; and if it is a good one, we'll applaud it. I don't see that we need concern ourselves further about the matter."

"It may be so," replied Cyrus Harding, "for the ancient track of the lava is still open; and thanks to this, the crater has hitherto overflowed towards the north. And yet—"

"And yet, as we can derive no advantage from an eruption, it might be better it should not take place," said the reporter.

"Who knows?" answered the sailor. "Perhaps there may be some valuable substance in this volcano, which it will spout forth, and which we may turn to good account!"

Cyrus Harding shook his head with the air of a man who augured no good from the phenomenon whose developments had been so sudden. He did not regard so lightly as Pencroft the results of an eruption. If the lava, in consequence of the position of the crater, did not directly menace the wooded and cultivated parts of the island, other complications might present themselves. In fact, eruptions are not unfrequently accompanied by earthquakes; and an island of the nature of Lincoln Island formed of substances so varied, basalt on one side, granite on the other, lava on the north, rich soil on the south, substances which consequently could not be firmly attached to each other, would be exposed to the risk of disintegration. Although, therefore, the spreading of the volcanic matter might not constitute a serious danger, any movement of the terrestrial structure which should shake the island might entail the gravest consequences.

"It seems to me," said Ayrton, who had reclined so as to place his ear to the ground, "it seems to me that I can hear a dull, rumbling sound, like that of a wagon loaded with bars of iron."

The colonists listened with the greatest attention, and were convinced that Ayrton was not mistaken. The rumbling was mingled with a subterranean roar, which formed a sort of *rinforzando*, and died slowly away, as if some violent storm had passed through the profundities of the globe. But no explosion, properly so termed, could be heard. It might therefore be concluded that the vapours and smoke found a free passage through the central shaft; and that the safety-valve being sufficiently large, no convulsion would be produced, no explosion was to be apprehended.

"Well, then!" said Pencroft, "are we not going back to work? Let Mount Franklin smoke, groan, bellow, or spout forth fire and flame as much as it pleases, that is no reason why we should be idle! Come, Ayrton, Neb, Herbert, Captain Harding, Mr. Spilett, every one of us must turn to at our work to-day! We are going to place the keelson, and a dozen pair of hands would not be too many. Before two months I want our new *Bonadventure*—for we shall keep the old name, shall we not?—to float on the waters of Port Balloon! Therefore there is not an hour to lose!"

All the colonists, their services thus requisitioned by Pencroft, descended to the dockyard, and proceeded to place the keelson, a thick mass of wood which forms the lower portion of a ship and unites firmly the timbers of the hull. It was an arduous undertaking, in which all took part.

They continued their labours during the whole of this day, the 3rd of January, without thinking further of the volcano, which could not, besides, be seen from the shore of Granite House. But once or twice, large shadows, veiling the sun, which described its diurnal arc through an extremely clear sky, indicated that a thick cloud of smoke passed between its disc and the island. The wind, blowing on the shore, carried all these vapours to the westward. Cyrus Harding and Gideon Spilett remarked these sombre appearances, and from time to time discussed the evident progress of the volcanic phenomena, but their work went on without interruption. It was, besides, of the first importance from every point of view, that the vessel should be finished with the least possible delay. In presence of the eventualities which might arise, the safety of the colonists would be to a great extent secured by their ship. Who could tell that it might not prove some day their only refuge?

In the evening, after supper, Cyrus Harding, Gideon Spilett, and Herbert, again ascended the plateau of Prospect Heights. It was already dark, and the obscurity would permit them to ascertain if flames or incandescent matter thrown up by the volcano were mingled with the vapour and smoke accumulated at the mouth of the crater.

"The crater is on fire!" said Herbert, who, more active than his companions, first reached the plateau.

Mount Franklin, distant about six miles, now appeared like a gigantic torch, around the summit of which turned fuliginous flames.

So much smoke, and possibly scoriae and cinders were mingled with them, that their light gleamed but faintly amid the gloom of the night. But a kind of lurid brilliancy spread over the island, against which stood out confusedly the wooded masses of the heights. Immense whirlwinds of vapour obscured the sky, through which glimmered a few stars.

"The change is rapid!" said the engineer. "That is not surprising," answered the reporter. "The re-awakening of the volcano already dates back some time. You may remember, Cyrus, that the first vapours appeared about the time we searched the sides of the mountain to discover Captain Nemo's retreat. It was, if I mistake not, about the 15th of October."

"Yes," replied Herbert, "two months and a half ago!"

"The subterranean fires have therefore been smouldering for ten weeks," resumed Gideon Spilett, "and it is not to be wondered at that they now break out with such violence!"

"Do not you feel a certain vibration of the soil?" asked Cyrus Harding.

"Yes," replied Gideon Spilett, "but there is a great difference between that and an earthquake."

"I do not affirm that we are menaced with an earthquake," answered Cyrus Harding, "may God preserve us from that! No; these vibrations are due to the effervescence of the central fire. The crust of the earth is simply the shell of a boiler, and you know that such a shell, under the pressure of steam, vibrates like a sonorous plate. It is this effect which is being produced at this moment."

"What magnificent flames!" exclaimed Herbert.

At this instant a kind of bouquet of flames shot forth from the crater, the brilliancy of which was visible even through the vapours. Thousands of luminous sheets and barbed tongues of fire were cast in various directions. Some, extending beyond the dome of smoke, dissipated it, leaving behind an incandescent powder. This was accompanied by successive explosions, resembling the discharge of a battery of mitrailleuses.

Cyrus Harding, the reporter, and Herbert, after spending an hour on the plateau of Prospect Heights, again descended to the beach, and returned to Granite House. The engineer was thoughtful and preoccupied, so much so, indeed, that Gideon Spilett inquired if he apprehended any immediate danger, of which the eruption might directly or indirectly be the cause.

"Yes, and no," answered Cyrus Harding.

"Nevertheless," continued the reporter, "would not the greatest misfortune which could happen to us be an earthquake which would overturn the island? Now, I do not suppose that this is to be feared, since the vapours and lava have found a free outlet."

"True," replied Cyrus Harding, "and I do not fear an earthquake in the sense in which the term is commonly applied to convulsions of the soil provoked by the expansion of subterranean gases. But other causes may produce great disasters."

"How so, my dear Cyrus?"

"I am not certain. I must consider. I must visit the mountain. In a few days I shall learn more on this point."

Gideon Spilett said no more, and soon, in spite of the explosions of the volcano, whose intensity increased, and which were repeated by the echoes of the island, the inhabitants of Granite House were sleeping soundly.

Three days passed by—the 4th, 5th, and 6th of January. The construction of the vessel was diligently continued, and without offering further explanations the engineer pushed forward the work with all his energy. Mount Franklin was now hooded by a sombre cloud of sinister aspect, and, amid the flames, vomited forth incandescent rocks, some of which fell back into the crater itself. This caused Pencroft, who would only look at the matter in the light of a joke, to exclaim—

"Ah! the giant is playing at cup and ball; he is a conjuror."

In fact, the substances thrown up fell back again into the abyss, and it did not seem that the lava, though swollen by the internal pressure, had yet risen to the orifice of the crater. At any rate, the opening on the north-east, which was partly visible, poured out no torrent upon the northern slope of the mountain.

Nevertheless, however pressing was the construction of the vessel, other duties demanded the presence of the colonists on various portions of the island. Before everything it was necessary to go to the corral, where the flocks of musmons and goats were enclosed, and replenish the provision of forage for those animals. It was accordingly arranged that Ayrton should proceed thither the next day, the 7th of January; and as he was sufficient for the task, to which he was accustomed, Pencroft and the rest were somewhat surprised on hearing the engineer say to Ayrton—

"As you are going to-morrow to the corral I will accompany you."

"But, Captain Harding," exclaimed the sailor, "our working days will not be many, and if you go also we shall be two pair of hands short!"

"We shall return to-morrow," replied Cyrus Harding, "but it is necessary that I should go to the corral. I must learn how the eruption is progressing."

"The eruption! always the eruption!" answered Pencroft, with an air of discontent. "An important thing, truly, this eruption! I trouble myself very little about it."

Whatever might be the sailor's opinion, the expedition projected by the engineer was settled for the next day. Herbert wished to accompany Cyrus Harding, but he would not vex Pencroft by his absence.

The next day, at dawn, Cyrus Harding and Ayrton, mounting the cart drawn by two onagas, took the road to the corral and set off at a round trot.

Above the forest were passing large clouds, to which the crater of Mount Franklin incessantly added fuliginous matter. These clouds, which rolled heavily in the air, were evidently composed of heterogeneous substances. It was not alone from the volcano that they derived their strange opacity and weight. Scorias, in a state of dust, like powdered pumice-stone, and greyish ashes as small as the finest feculae, were held in suspension in the midst of their thick folds. These ashes are so fine that they have been observed in the air for whole months. After the eruption of 1783 in Iceland for upwards of a year the atmosphere was thus charged with volcanic dust through which the rays of the sun were only with difficulty discernible.

But more often this pulverised matter falls, and this happened on the present occasion. Cyrus Harding and Ayrton had scarcely reached the corral when a sort of black snow like fine gunpowder fell, and instantly changed the appearance of the soil. Trees, meadows, all disappeared beneath a covering several inches in depth. But, very fortunately, the wind blew from the north-east, and the greater part of the cloud dissolved itself over the sea.

"This is very singular, Captain Harding," said Ayrton.

"It is very serious," replied the engineer. "This powdered pumice-stone, all this mineral dust, proves how grave is the convulsion going forward in the lower depths of the volcano."

"But can nothing be done?"

"Nothing, except to note the progress of the phenomenon. Do you, therefore, Ayrton, occupy yourself with the necessary work at the corral. In the meantime I will ascend just beyond the source of Red Creek and examine the condition of the mountain upon its northern aspect. Then—"

"Well, Captain Harding?"

"Then we will pay a visit to Dakkar Grotto. I wish to inspect it. At any rate I will come back for you in two hours."

Ayrton then proceeded to enter the corral, and, while waiting the engineer's return, busied himself with the musmons and goats, which seemed to feel a certain uneasiness in presence of these first signs of an eruption.

Meanwhile Cyrus Harding ascended the crest of the eastern spur, passed Red Creek, and arrived at the spot where he and his companions had discovered a sulphureous spring at the time of their first exploration.

How changed was everything! Instead of a single column of smoke he counted thirteen, forced through the soil as if violently propelled by some piston. It was evident that the crust of the earth was subjected in this part of the globe to a frightful pressure. The atmosphere was saturated with gases and carbonic acid, mingled with aqueous vapours. Cyrus Harding felt the volcanic tufa with which the plain was strewn, and which were but pulverised cinders hardened into solid blocks by time, tremble beneath him, but he could discover no traces of fresh lava.

The engineer became more assured of this when he observed all the northern part of Mount Franklin. Pillars of smoke and flame escaped from the crater; a hail of scorias fell on the ground; but no current of lava burst from the mouth of the volcano, which proved that the volcanic matter had not yet attained the level of the superior orifice of the central shaft.

"But I would prefer that it were so," said Cyrus Harding to himself. "At any rate, I should then know that the lava had followed its accustomed track. Who can say that they may not take a new course? But the danger does not consist in that! Captain Nemo foresaw it clearly! No, the danger does not lie there!"

Cyrus Harding advanced towards the enormous causeway whose prolongation enclosed the narrow Shark Gulf. He could now sufficiently examine on this side the ancient channels of the lava. There was no doubt in his mind that the most recent eruption had occurred at a far-distant epoch.

He then returned by the same way, listening attentively to the subterranean mutterings which rolled like long-continued thunder, interrupted by deafening explosions. At nine in the morning he reached the corral.

Ayrton awaited him.

JULES VERNE (TRANSLATION FROM W.H.G. KINGSTON)

"The animals are cared for, Captain Harding," said Ayrton.

"Good, Ayrton."

"They seem uneasy, Captain Harding."

"Yes, instinct speaks through them, and instinct is never deceived."

"Are you ready?"

"Take a lamp, Ayrton," answered the engineer; "we will start at once."

Ayrton did as desired. The onagas, unharnessed, roamed in the corral. The gate was secured on the outside, and Cyrus Harding, preceding Ayrton, took the narrow path which led westward to the shore.

The soil they walked upon was choked with the pulverised matter fallen from the cloud. No quadruped appeared in the woods. Even the birds had fled. Sometimes a passing breeze raised the covering of ashes, and the two colonists, enveloped in a whirlwind of dust, lost sight of each other. They were then careful to cover their eyes and mouths with handkerchiefs, for they ran the risk of being blinded and suffocated.

It was impossible for Cyrus Harding and Ayrton, with these impediments, to make rapid progress. Moreover, the atmosphere was close, as if the oxygen had been partly burnt up, and had become unfit for respiration. At every hundred paces they were obliged to stop to take breath. It was therefore past ten o'clock when the engineer and his companion reached the crest of the enormous mass of rocks of basalt and porphyry which composed the north-west coast of the island.

Ayrton and Cyrus Harding commenced the descent of this abrupt declivity, following almost step for step the difficult path which, during that stormy night, had led them to Dakkar Grotto. In open day the descent was less perilous, and, besides, the bed of ashes which covered the polished surface of the rock enabled them to make their footing more secure.

The ridge at the end of the shore, about forty feet in height, was soon reached. Cyrus Harding recollected that this elevation gradually sloped towards the level of the sea. Although the tide was at present low, no beach could be seen, and the waves, thickened by the volcanic dust, beat upon the basaltic rocks.

Cyrus Harding and Ayrton found without difficulty the entrance to Dakkar Grotto, and paused for a moment at the last rock before it.

"The iron boat should be there," said the engineer.

"It is here, Captain Harding," replied Ayrton, drawing towards him the fragile craft, which was protected by the arch of a vault.

"On board, Ayrton!"

The two colonists stepped into the boat. A slight undulation of the waves carried it farther under the low arch of the crypt, and there Ayrton, with the aid of flint and steel, lighted the lamp. He then took the oars, and the lamp having been placed in the bow of the boat, so that its rays fell before them, Cyrus Harding took the helm and steered through the shades of the grotto.

The *Nautilus* was there no longer to illuminate the cavern with its electric light. Possibly it might not yet be extinguished, but no ray escaped from the depths of the abyss in which reposed all that was mortal of Captain Nemo.

The light afforded by the lamp, although feeble, nevertheless enabled the engineer to advance slowly, following the wall of the cavern. A deathlike silence reigned under the vaulted roof, or at least in the anterior portion, for soon Cyrus Harding distinctly heard the rumbling which proceeded from the bowels of the mountain.

"That comes from the volcano," he said.

Besides these sounds, the presence of chemical combinations was soon betrayed by their powerful odour, and the engineer and his companion were almost suffocated by sulphureous vapours.

"This is what Captain Nemo feared," murmured Cyrus Harding, changing countenance. "We must go to the end, notwithstanding."

"Forward!" replied Ayrton, bending to his oars and directing the boat towards the head of the cavern.

Twenty-five minutes after entering the mouth of the grotto the boat reached the extreme end.

Cyrus Harding then, standing up, cast the light of the lamp upon the walls of the cavern which separated it from the central shaft of the volcano. What was the thickness of this wall? It might be ten feet or a hundred feet—it was impossible to say. But the subterranean sounds were too perceptible to allow of the supposition that it was of any great thickness.

The engineer, after having explored the wall at a certain height horizontally, fastened the lamp to the end of an oar, and again surveyed the basaltic wall at a greater elevation.

There, through scarcely visible clefts and joinings, escaped a pungent vapour, which infected the atmosphere of the cavern. The wall was broken by large cracks, some of which extended to within two or three feet of the water's edge.

Cyrus Harding thought for a brief space. Then he said in a low voice—

"Yes! the captain was right! The danger lies there, and a terrible danger!"

Ayrton said not a word, but, upon a sign from Cyrus Harding, resumed the oars, and half an hour later the engineer and he reached the entrance of Dakkar Grotto.

XIX

Cyrus Harding gives an Account of his Exploration—
The Construction of the Ship pushed forward—A Last Visit
to the Corral—The Battle between Fire and Water—
All that remains of the Island—It is decided to Launch
the Vessel—The Night of the 8th of March.

The next day, the 8th of January, after a day and night passed at the corral, where they left all in order, Cyrus Harding and Ayrton arrived at Granite House.

The engineer immediately called his companions together, and informed them of the imminent danger which threatened Lincoln Island, and from which no human power could deliver them.

"My friends," he said, and his voice betrayed the depth of his emotion, "our island is not among those which will endure while this earth endures. It is doomed to more or less speedy destruction, the cause of which it bears within itself, and from which nothing can save it."

The colonists looked at each other, then at the engineer. They did not clearly comprehend him.

"Explain yourself, Cyrus!" said Gideon Spilett.

"I will do so," replied Cyrus Harding, "or rather I will simply afford you the explanation which, during our few minutes of private conversation, was given me by Captain Nemo."

"Captain Nemo!" exclaimed the colonists.

"Yes, and it was the last service he desired to render us before his death!"

"The last service!" exclaimed Pencroft, "the last service! You will see that though he is dead he will render us others yet!"

"But what did the captain say?" inquired the reporter.

"I will tell you, my friends," said the engineer. "Lincoln Island does not resemble the other islands of the Pacific, and a fact of which Captain Nemo has made me cognisant must sooner or later bring about the subversion of its foundation."

"Nonsense! Lincoln Island, it can't be!" cried Pencroft, who, in spite of the respect he felt for Cyrus Harding, could not prevent a gesture of incredulity.

"Listen, Pencroft," resumed the engineer, "I will tell you what Captain

Nemo communicated to me, and which I myself confirmed yesterday, during the exploration of Dakkar Grotto. This cavern stretches under the island as far as the volcano, and is only separated from its central shaft by the wall which terminates it. Now, this wall is seamed with fissures and clefts which already allow the sulphureous gases generated in the interior of the volcano to escape."

"Well?" said Pencroft, his brow suddenly contracting.

"Well, then, I saw that these fissures widen under the internal pressure from within, that the wall of basalt is gradually giving way, and that after a longer or shorter period it will afford a passage to the waters of the lake which fill the cavern."

"Good!" replied Pencroft, with an attempt at pleasantry. "The sea will extinguish the volcano, and there will be an end of the matter!"

"Not so!" said Cyrus Harding, "should a day arrive when the sea, rushing through the wall of the cavern, penetrates by the central shaft into the interior of the island to the boiling lava, Lincoln Island will that day be blown into the air—just as would happen to the island of Sicily were the Mediterranean to precipitate itself into Mount Etna."

The colonists made no answer to these significant words of the engineer. They now understood the danger by which they were menaced.

It may be added that Cyrus Harding had in no way exaggerated the danger to be apprehended. Many persons have formed an idea that it would be possible to extinguish volcanoes, which are almost always situated on the shores of a sea or lake, by opening a passage for the admission of the water. But they are not aware that this would be to incur the risk of blowing up a portion of the globe, like a boiler whose steam is suddenly expanded by intense heat. The water, rushing into a cavity whose temperature might be estimated at thousands of degrees, would be converted into steam with a sudden energy which no enclosure could resist.

It was not therefore doubtful that the island, menaced by a frightful and approaching convulsion, would endure only so long as the wall of Dakkar Grotto itself should endure. It was not even a question of months, nor of weeks; but of days, it might be of hours.

The first sentiment which the colonists felt was that of profound sorrow. They thought not so much of the peril which menaced themselves personally, but of the destruction of the island which had sheltered them, which they had cultivated, which they loved so well, and had hoped to render so flourishing. So much effort ineffectually expended, so much labour lost.

Pencroft could not prevent a large tear from rolling down his cheek, nor did he attempt to conceal it.

Some further conversation now took place. The chances yet in favour of the colonists were discussed; but finally it was agreed that there was not an hour to be lost, that the building and fitting of the vessel should be pushed forward with their utmost energy, and that this was the sole chance of safety for the inhabitants of Lincoln Island.

All hands, therefore, set to work on the vessel. What could it now avail to sow, to reap, to hunt, to increase the stores of Granite House? The contents of the store-house and outbuildings contained more than sufficient to provide the ship for a voyage, however long might be its duration. But it was imperative that the ship should be ready to receive them before the inevitable catastrophe should arrive.

Their labours were now carried on with feverish ardour. By the 23rd of January the vessel was half-decked over. Up to this time no change had taken place in the summit of the volcano. Vapour and smoke mingled with flames and incandescent stones were thrown up from the crater. But during the night of the 23rd, in consequence of the lava attaining the level of the first stratum of the volcano, the hat-shaped cone which formed over the latter disappeared. A frightful sound was heard. The colonists at first thought the island was rent asunder, and rushed out of Granite House.

This occurred about two o'clock in the morning.

The sky appeared on fire. The superior cone, a mass of rock a thousand feet in height, and weighing thousands of millions of pounds, had been thrown down upon the island, making it tremble to its foundation. Fortunately, this cone inclined to the north, and had fallen upon the plain of sand and tufa stretching between the volcano and the sea. The aperture of the crater being thus enlarged projected towards the sky a glare so intense that by the simple effect of reflection the atmosphere appeared red-hot. At the same time a torrent of lava, bursting from the new summit, poured out in long cascades, like water escaping from a vase too full, and a thousand tongues of fire crept over the sides of the volcano.

"The corral! the corral!" exclaimed Ayrton.

It was, in fact, towards the corral that the lava was rushing, as the new crater faced the east, and consequently the fertile portions of the island, the springs of Red Creek and Jacamar Wood, were menaced with instant destruction.

At Ayrton's cry the colonists rushed to the onagas' stables. The cart was at once harnessed. All were possessed by the same thought—to hasten to the corral and set at liberty the animals it enclosed.

Before three in the morning they arrived at the corral. The cries of the terrified musmons and goats indicated the alarm which possessed them. Already a torrent of burning matter and liquefied minerals fell from the side of the mountain upon the meadows as far as the side of the palisade. The gate was burst open by Ayrton, and the animals, bewildered with terror, fled in all directions.

An hour afterwards the boiling lava filled the corral, converting into vapour the water of the little rivulet which ran through it, burning up the house like dry grass, and leaving not even a post of the palisade to mark the spot where the corral once stood.

To contend against this disaster would have been folly—nay, madness. In presence of Nature's grand convulsions man is powerless.

It was now daylight—the 24th of January. Cyrus Harding and his companions, before returning to Granite House, desired to ascertain the probable direction this inundation of lava was about to take. The soil sloped gradually from Mount Franklin to the east coast, and it was to be feared that, in spite of the thick Jacamar Wood, the torrent would reach the plateau of Prospect Heights.

"The lake will cover us," said Gideon Spilett.

"I hope so!" was Cyrus Harding's only reply.

The colonists were desirous of reaching the plain upon which the superior cone of Mount Franklin had fallen, but the lava arrested their progress. It had followed, on one side, the valley of Red Creek, and on the other that of Falls River, evaporating those watercourses in its passage. There was no possibility of crossing the torrent of lava; on the contrary, the colonists were obliged to retreat before it. The volcano, without its crown, was no longer recognisable, terminated as it was by a sort of flat table which replaced the ancient crater. From two openings in its southern and eastern sides an unceasing flow of lava poured forth, thus forming two distinct streams. Above the new crater a cloud of smoke and ashes, mingled with those of the atmosphere, massed over the island. Loud peals of thunder broke, and could scarcely be distinguished from the rumblings of the mountain, whose mouth vomited forth ignited rocks, which, hurled to more than a thousand feet, burst in the air like shells. Flashes of lightning rivalled in intensity the volcano's eruption.

Towards seven in the morning the position was no longer tenable by the colonists, who accordingly took shelter in the borders of Jacamar Wood. Not only did the projectiles begin to rain around them, but the lava, overflowing the bed of Red Creek, threatened to cut off the road to the corral. The nearest rows of trees caught fire, and their sap, suddenly transformed into vapour, caused them to explode with loud reports, whilst others, less moist, remained unhurt in the midst of the inundation.

The colonists had again taken the road to the corral. They proceeded but slowly, frequently looking back; but, in consequence of the inclination of the soil, the lava gained rapidly in the east, and as its lower waves became solidified, others at boiling heat covered them immediately.

Meanwhile, the principal stream of Red Creek valley became more and more menacing. All this portion of the forest was on fire, and enormous wreaths of smoke rolled over the trees, whose trunks were already consumed by the lava. The colonists halted near the lake, about half a mile from the mouth of Red Creek. A question of life or death was now to be decided.

Cyrus Harding, accustomed to the consideration of important crises, and aware that he was addressing men capable of hearing the truth, whatever it might be, then said—

"Either the lake will arrest the progress of the lava, and a part of the island will be preserved from utter destruction, or the stream will overrun the forests of the Far West, and not a tree or plant will remain on the surface of the soil. We shall have no prospect but that of starvation upon these barren rocks—a death which will probably be anticipated by the explosion of the island."

"In that case," replied Pencroft, folding his arms and stamping his foot, "what's the use of working any longer on the vessel?"

"Pencroft," answered Cyrus Harding, "we must do our duty to the last!"

At this instant the river of lava, after having broken a passage through the noble trees it devoured in its course, reached the borders of the lake. At this point there was an elevation of the soil which, had it been greater, might have sufficed to arrest the torrent.

"To work!" cried Cyrus Harding.

The engineer's thought was at once understood. It might be possible to dam, as it were, the torrent, and thus compel it to pour itself into the lake.

The colonists hastened to the dockyard. They returned with shovels, picks, axes, and by means of banking the earth with the aid of fallen trees they succeeded in a few hours in raising an embankment three feet high and some hundreds of paces in length. It seemed to them, when they had finished, as if they had scarcely been working more than a few minutes.

It was not a moment too soon. The liquefied substances soon after reached the bottom of the barrier. The stream of lava swelled like a river about to overflow its banks, and threatened to demolish the sole obstacle which could prevent it from overrunning the whole Far West. But the dam held firm, and after a moment of terrible suspense the torrent precipitated itself into Grant Lake from a height of twenty feet.

The colonists, without moving or uttering a word, breathlessly regarded this strife of the two elements.

What a spectacle was this conflict between water and fire! What pen could describe the marvellous horror of this scene—what pencil could depict it? The water hissed as it evaporated by contact with the boiling lava. The vapour whirled in the air to an immeasurable height, as if the valves of an immense boiler had been suddenly opened. But, however considerable might be the volume of water contained in the lake, it must eventually be absorbed, because it was not replenished, whilst the stream of lava, fed from an inexhaustible source, rolled on without ceasing new waves of incandescent matter.

The first waves of lava which fell in the lake immediately solidified, and accumulated so as speedily to emerge from it. Upon their surface fell other waves, which in their turn became stone, but a step nearer the centre of the lake. In this manner was formed a pier which threatened to gradually fill up the lake, which could not overflow, the water displaced by the lava being evaporated. The hissing of the water rent the air with a deafening sound, and the vapour, blown by the wind, fell in rain upon the sea. The pier became longer and longer, and the blocks of lava piled themselves one on another. Where formerly stretched the calm waters of the lake now appeared an enormous mass of smoking rocks, as if an upheaving of the soil had formed immense shoals. Imagine the waters of the lake aroused by a hurricane, then suddenly solidified by an intense frost, and some conception may be formed of the aspect of the lake three hours after the irruption of this irresistible torrent of lava.

This time water would be vanquished by fire.

Nevertheless it was a fortunate circumstance for the colonists that the effusion of lava should have been in the direction of Lake Grant. They had before them some days' respite. The plateau of Prospect Heights, Granite House, and the dockyard were for the moment preserved. And these few days it was necessary to employ them in planking, carefully caulking the vessel, and launching her. The colonists would then take refuge on board the vessel, content to rig her after she should be afloat on the waters. With the danger of an explosion which threatened to destroy the island there could be no security on shore. The walls of Granite House, once so sure a retreat, might at any moment fall in upon them.

During the six following days, from the 25th to the 30th of January, the colonists accomplished as much of the construction of their vessel as twenty men could have done. They hardly allowed themselves a moment's repose, and the glare of the flames which shot from the crater enabled them to work night and day. The flow of lava continued, but perhaps less abundantly. This was fortunate, for Lake Grant was almost entirely choked up, and if more lava should accumulate it would inevitably spread over the plateau of Prospect Heights, and thence upon the beach.

But if the island was thus partially protected on this side, it was not so with the western part.

In fact, the second stream of lava, which had followed the valley of Falls River, a valley of great extent, the land on both sides of the creek being flat, met with no obstacle. The burning liquid had then spread through the forest of the Far West. At this period of the year, when the trees were dried up by a tropical heat, the forest caught fire instantaneously, in such a manner that the conflagration extended itself both by the trunks of the trees and by their higher branches, whose interlacement favoured its progress. It even appeared that the current of flame spread more rapidly among the summits of the trees than the current of lava at their bases.

Thus it happened that the wild animals, jaguars, wild boars, cabybaras, koulas, and game of every kind, mad with terror, had fled to the banks of the Mercy and to the Tadorn Marsh, beyond the road to Port Balloon. But the colonists were too much occupied with their task to pay any attention to even the most formidable of these animals. They had abandoned Granite House, and would not even take shelter at the Chimneys, but encamped under a tent, near the mouth of the Mercy.

Each day Cyrus Harding and Gideon Spilett ascended the plateau of Prospect Heights. Sometimes Herbert accompanied them, but never Pencroft, who could not bear to look upon the prospect of the island now so utterly devastated.

It was, in truth, a heartrending spectacle. All the wooded part of the island was now completely bare. One single clump of green trees raised their heads at the extremity of Serpentine Peninsula. Here and there were a few grotesque blackened and branchless stumps. The site of the devastated forest was even more barren than Tadorn Marsh. The irruption of the lava had been complete. Where formerly sprang up that charming verdure, the soil was now nothing but a savage mass of volcanic tufa. In the valleys of the Falls and Mercy rivers no drop of water now flowed towards the sea, and should Lake Grant be entirely dried up, the colonists would have no means of quenching their thirst. But, fortunately, the lava had spared the southern corner of the lake, containing all that remained of the drinkable water of the island. Towards the north-west stood out the rugged and well-defined outlines of the sides of the volcano, like a gigantic claw hovering over the island. What a sad and fearful sight, and how painful to the colonists, who, from a fertile domain covered with forests, irrigated by watercourses, and enriched by the produce of their toils, found themselves, as it were, transported to a desolate rock, upon which, but for their reserves of provisions, they could not even gather the means of subsistence!

"It is enough to break one's heart!" said Gideon Spilett, one day.

"Yes, Spilett," answered the engineer. "May God grant us the time to complete this vessel, now our sole refuge!"

"Do not you think, Cyrus, that the violence of the eruption has somewhat lessened? The volcano still vomits forth lava, but somewhat less abundantly, if I mistake not."

"It matters little," answered Cyrus Harding. "The fire is still burning in the interior of the mountain, and the sea may break in at any moment. We are in the condition of passengers whose ship is devoured by a conflagration which they cannot extinguish, and who know that sooner or later the flames must reach the powder-magazine. To work, Spilett, to work, and let us not lose an hour!"

During eight days more, that is to say until the 7th of February, the lava continued to flow, but the eruption was confined within the previous limits. Cyrus Harding feared above all lest the liquefied matter should overflow the shore, for in that event the dockyard could not escape. Moreover, about this time the colonists felt in the frame of the island vibrations which alarmed them to the highest degree.

It was the 20th of February. Yet another month must elapse before the vessel would be ready for sea. Would the island hold together till then? The intention of Pencroft and Cyrus Harding was to launch the vessel as soon as the hull should be complete. The deck, the upper-works, the interior woodwork and the rigging, might be finished afterwards, but the essential point was that the colonists should have an assured refuge away from the island. Perhaps it might be even better to conduct the vessel to Port Balloon, that is to say, as far as possible from the centre of eruption, for at the mouth of the Mercy, between the islet and the wall of granite, it would run the risk of being crushed in the event of any convulsion. All the exertions of the voyagers were therefore concentrated upon the completion of the hull.

Thus the 3rd of March arrived, and they might calculate upon launching the vessel in ten days.

Hope revived in the hearts of the colonists, who had, in this fourth year of their sojourn on Lincoln Island, suffered so many trials. Even Pencroft lost in some measure the sombre taciturnity occasioned by the devastation and ruin of his domain. His hopes, it is true, were concentrated upon his vessel.

"We shall finish it," he said to the engineer, "we shall finish it, captain, and it is time, for the season is advancing and the equinox will soon be here. Well, if necessary, we must put in to Tabor Island to spend the winter. But think of Tabor Island after Lincoln Island. Ah, how unfortunate! Who could have believed it possible?"

"Let us get on," was the engineer's invariable reply.

And they worked away without losing a moment.

"Master," asked Neb, a few days later, "do you think all this could have happened if Captain Nemo had been still alive?"

"Certainly, Neb," answered Cyrus Harding.

"I, for one, don't believe it!" whispered Pencroft to Neb.

"Nor I!" answered Neb seriously.

During the first week of March appearances again became menacing. Thousands of threads like glass, formed of fluid lava, fell like rain upon the island. The crater was again boiling with lava which overflowed the back of the volcano. The torrent flowed along the surface of the hardened tufa, and destroyed the few meagre skeletons of trees which had withstood the first eruption. The stream flowing this time towards the south-west shore of Lake Grant, stretched beyond Creek Glycerine, and invaded the plateau of Prospect Heights. This last blow to the work of the colonists was terrible. The mill, the buildings of the inner court, the stables, were all destroyed. The affrighted poultry fled in all directions. Top and Jup showed signs of the greatest alarm, as if their instinct warned them of an impending catastrophe. A large number of the animals of the island had perished in the first eruption. Those which survived found no refuge but Tadorn Marsh, save a few to which the plateau of Prospect Heights afforded an asylum. But even this last retreat was now closed to them, and the lava-torrent, flowing over the edge of the granite wall, began to pour down upon the beach its cataracts of fire. The sublime horror of this spectacle passed all description. During the night it could only be compared to a Niagara of molten fluid, with its incandescent vapours above and its boiling masses below.

The colonists were driven to their last entrenchment, and although the upper seams of the vessel were not yet caulked, they decided to launch her at once.

Pencroft and Ayrton therefore set about the necessary preparations for the launch, which was to take place the morning of the next day, the 9th of March.

But, during the night of the 8th an enormous column of vapour escaping from the crater rose with frightful explosions to a height of more than three thousand feet. The wall of Dakkar Grotto had evidently given way under the pressure of the gases, and the sea, rushing through the central shaft into the igneous gulf, was at once converted into vapour. But the crater could not afford a sufficient outlet for this vapour. An explosion, which might have been heard at a distance of a hundred miles, shook the air. Fragments of mountains fell into the Pacific, and, in a few minutes, the ocean rolled over the spot where Lincoln Island once stood.

XX

An Isolated Rock in the Pacific—The last Refuge of the
Colonists of Lincoln Island—Death their only
Prospect—Unexpected Succour—Why and how it
Arrives—A Last Kindness—An Island on Terra Firma—
The Tomb of Captain Prince Dakkar Nemo.

An isolated rock, thirty feet in length, twenty in breadth, scarcely ten from the water's edge, such was the only solid point which the waves of the Pacific had not engulfed.

It was all that remained of the structure of Granite House! The wall had fallen headlong and been then shattered to fragments, and a few of the rocks of the large room were piled one above another to form this point. All around had disappeared in the abyss; the inferior cone of Mount Franklin, rent asunder by the explosion; the lava jaws of Shark Gulf, the plateau of Prospect Heights, Safety Islet, the granite rocks of Port Balloon, the basalts of Dakkar Grotto, the long Serpentine Peninsula, so distant nevertheless from the centre of the eruption. All that could now be seen of Lincoln Island was the narrow rock which now served as a refuge to the six colonists and their dog Top.

The animals had also perished in the catastrophe; the birds, as well as those representing the fauna of the island—all either crushed or drowned, and the unfortunate Jup himself had, alas! found his death in some crevice of the soil.

If Cyrus Harding, Gideon Spilett, Herbert, Pencroft, Neb, and Ayrton had survived, it was because, assembled under their tent, they had been hurled into the sea at the instant when the fragments of the island rained down on every side.

When they reached the surface they could only perceive, at half a cable's length, this mass of rocks, towards which they swam and on which they found footing.

On this barren rock they had now existed for nine days. A few provisions taken from the magazine of Granite House before the catastrophe, a little fresh water from the rain which had fallen in a hollow of the rock, was all that the unfortunate colonists possessed. Their last hope, the vessel, had been shattered to pieces. They had no means of quitting the reef; no fire, nor any means of obtaining it. It seemed that they must inevitably perish.

This day, the 18th of March, there remained only provisions for two days, although they limited their consumption to the bare necessaries of life. All their science and intelligence could avail them nothing in their present position. They were in the hand of God.

Cyrus Harding was calm, Gideon Spilett more nervous, and Pencroft, a prey to sullen anger, walked to and fro on the rock. Herbert did not for a moment quit the engineer's side as if demanding from him that assistance he had no power to give. Neb and Ayrton were resigned to their fate.

"Ah, what a misfortune! what a misfortune!" often repeated Pencroft. "If we had but a walnut-shell to take us to Tabor Island! But we have nothing, nothing!"

"Captain Nemo did right to die," said Neb.

During the five ensuing days Cyrus Harding and his unfortunate companions husbanded their provisions with the most extreme care, eating only what would prevent them from succumbing to starvation. Their weakness was extreme. Herbert and Neb began to show symptoms of delirium.

Under these circumstances was it possible for them to retain even the shadow of a hope? No! What was their sole remaining chance? That a vessel should appear in sight off the rock? But they knew only too well from experience that no ships ever visited this part of the Pacific. Could they calculate that, by a truly providential coincidence, the Scotch yacht would arrive precisely at this time in search of Ayrton at Tabor Island? It was scarcely probable; and, besides, supposing she should come there, as the colonists had not been able to deposit a notice pointing out Ayrton's change of abode, the commander of the yacht, after having explored Tabor Island without result, would again set sail and return to lower latitudes.

No! no hope of being saved could be retained, and a horrible death, death from hunger and thirst, awaited them upon this rock.

Already they were stretched on the rock, inanimate, and no longer conscious of what passed around them. Ayrton alone, by a supreme effort, from time to time raised his head, and cast a despairing glance over the desert ocean.

But on the morning of the 24th of March Ayrton's arms were extended towards a point in the horizon; he raised himself, at first on his knees, then upright, and his hand seemed to make a signal.

A sail was in sight off the rock. She was evidently not without an object. The reef was the mark for which she was making in a direct line, under all steam, and the unfortunate colonists might have made her out some hours before if they had had the strength to watch the horizon.

"The *Duncan*!" murmured Ayrton—and fell back without sign of life.

When Cyrus Harding and his companions recovered consciousness, thanks to the attention lavished upon them, they found themselves in the cabin of a steamer, without being able to comprehend how they had escaped death.

A word from Ayrton explained everything.

"The *Duncan*!" he murmured.

"The *Duncan*!" exclaimed Cyrus Harding. And raising his hand to Heaven, he said, "Oh! Almighty God! mercifully hast Thou preserved us!"

It was, in fact, the *Duncan*, Lord Glenarvan's yacht, now commanded by Robert, son of Captain Grant, who had been despatched to Tabor Island to find Ayrton, and bring him back to his native land after twelve years of expiation.

The colonists were not only saved, but already on the way to their native country.

"Captain Grant," asked Cyrus Harding, "who can have suggested to you the idea, after having left Tabor Island, where you did not find Ayrton, of coming a hundred miles farther north-east?"

"Captain Harding," replied Robert Grant, "it was in order to find, not only Ayrton, but yourself and your companions."

"My companions and myself?"

"Doubtless, at Lincoln Island."

"At Lincoln Island!" exclaimed in a breath Gideon Spilett, Herbert, Neb, and Pencroft, in the highest degree astonished.

"How could you be aware of the existence of Lincoln Island?" inquired Cyrus Harding, "it is not even named in the charts."

"I knew of it from a document left by you on Tabor Island," answered Robert Grant.

"A document?" cried Gideon Spilett.

"Without doubt, and here it is," answered Robert Grant, producing a paper which indicated the longitude and latitude of Lincoln Island, "the present residence of Ayrton and five American colonists."

"It is Captain Nemo!" cried Cyrus Harding, after having read the notice, and recognised that the handwriting was similar to that of the paper found at the corral.

"Ah!" said Pencroft, "it was then he who took our *Bonadventure* and hazarded himself alone to go to Tabor Island!"

"In order to leave this notice," added Herbert.

"I was then right in saying," exclaimed the sailor, "that even after his death the captain would render us a last service."

"My friends," said Cyrus Harding, in a voice of the profoundest emotion, "may the God of mercy have had pity on the soul of Captain Nemo, our benefactor!"

The colonists uncovered themselves at these last words of Cyrus Harding, and murmured the name of Captain Nemo.

Then Ayrton, approaching the engineer, said simply, "Where should this coffer be deposited?"

It was the coffer which Ayrton had saved at the risk of his life, at the very instant that the island had been engulfed, and which he now faithfully handed to the engineer.

"Ayrton! Ayrton!" said Cyrus Harding, deeply touched. Then, addressing Robert Grant, "Sir," he added, "you left behind you a criminal; you find in his place a man who has become honest by penitence, and whose hand I am proud to clasp in mine."

Robert Grant was now made acquainted with the strange history of Captain Nemo and the colonists of Lincoln Island. Then, observations being taken of what remained of this shoal, which must henceforward figure on the charts of the Pacific, the order was given to make all sail.

A few weeks afterwards the colonists landed in America, and found their country once more at peace after the terrible conflict in which right and justice had triumphed.

Of the treasures contained in the coffer left by Captain Nemo to the colonists of Lincoln Island, the larger portion was employed in the purchase of a vast territory in the State of Iowa. One pearl alone, the finest, was reserved from the treasure and sent to Lady Glenarvan in the name of the castaways restored to their country by the *Duncan*.

There, upon this domain, the colonists invited to labour, that is to say, to wealth and happiness, all those to whom they had hoped to offer the hospitality of Lincoln Island. There was founded a vast colony to which they gave the name of that island sunk beneath the waters of the Pacific. A river was there called the Mercy, a mountain took the name of Mount Franklin, a small lake was named Lake Grant, and the forests became the forests of the Far West. It might have been an island on terra firma.

There, under the intelligent hands of the engineer and his companions, everything prospered. Not one of the former colonists of Lincoln Island was absent, for they had sworn to live always together. Neb was with his master; Ayrton was there ready to sacrifice himself for all; Pencroft was more a farmer than he had even been a sailor; Herbert, who completed his studies under the superintendence of Cyrus Harding; and Gideon Spilett, who founded the *New Lincoln Herald*, the best-informed journal in the world.

There Cyrus Harding and his companions received at intervals visits from Lord and Lady Glenarvan, Captain John Mangles and his wife, the sister of Robert Grant, Robert Grant himself, Major McNab, and all those who had taken part in the history both of Captain Grant and Captain Nemo.

There, to conclude, all were happy, united in the present as they had been in the past; but never could they forget that island upon which they had arrived poor and friendless, that island which, during four years, had supplied all their wants, and of which there remained but a fragment of granite washed by the waves of the Pacific, the tomb of him who had borne the name of Captain Nemo.

FINIS

bookfinity™

Discover more of your favorite classics with Bookfinity™.

- Track your reading with custom book lists.
- Get great book recommendations for your personalized Reader Type.
- Add reviews for your favorite books.
- AND MUCH MORE!

Visit **bookfinity.com** and take the fun Reader Type quiz to get started.

Enjoy our classic and modern companion pairings!

Classic & Modern